# The Load

D0556274

# The Load
## An Over-the-Road Mystery

Doug White

**G.R.U.B. Publishing Company**
Amherst, New York

This book is a work of fiction. Names, characters, and events are products of the author's imagination or are used fictitiously. Any resemblance to actual events or persons, living or deceased, is purely coincidental. We assume no responsibility for errors, inaccuracies, omissions, or any inconsistency herein.

First printing 2003

ISBN 0-9724334-4-9
LCCN 2002112927

**ATTENTION CORPORATIONS, UNIVERSITIES, COLLEGES, AND PROFESSIONAL ORGANIZATIONS:** Quantity discounts are available on bulk purchases of this book for educational, gift purposes, or as premiums for increasing magazine subscriptions or renewals. Special books or book excerpts can also be created to fit specific needs. For information, please contact G.R.U.B. Publishing Company, P.O. Box 179, Amherst, NY 14226; 866-738-4316 pin 0470.

This book is dedicated to the loving memory of Fred H. White, my father. Literally on his deathbed I read the portion of the book I had completed at that time and promised I would complete it.

## ACKNOWLEDGMENTS

Remembering who helped and encouraged me during the writing of this book is no problem, but listing them in order of importance is impossible. I've listed them in alphabetical order, hoping I would not slight anybody. In his or her own way everybody was equally important.

When I first came up with the idea for this story, all I knew for sure was that I wanted it to take place in Montana. I picked the town of Basin on the map for the jumping-off place to Slippery Gulch, hoping it would be suitable. Months later I was able to visit the town and talk with several residents. It was perfect. As I describe it in the book, "It's a long way from Broadway." There's even a little dirt road that runs out of town and up into the mountains where it leads off to different mines. The people gave me much of my information about the area. The citizens of Basin in the book are all fictitious but not unlike some real ones who live there.

The first time I ever owned a computer was to write this book. My nephew, Karl Biedlingmaier, was there by phone to get me back on track every time I pushed the wrong button—which was often. Not once did he ever call me stupid.

As a former teacher who taught primarily science and stayed as far away from English usage as I could, I relied on two old friends: Doug Denbow and Beth Friedman were my usage watchdogs, catching most of my errors in the draft.

While in Montana, I visited the Dillon Museum in Dillon, Montana, and the World Museum of Mining in Butte, Montana. I learned a lot about mining and the way the materials were transported at the turn of the century. All I can say is thank God for big truck air and jake brakes.

As I travel around the country in my big truck I talk to many other truck drivers. Many have given me ideas and suggestions. For instance, early in the book I was really stuck. I knew where I wanted to go in my story but I was getting there way too early. One particular driver suggested the idea of introducing a new character anytime I got stuck; thus, the "birth" of Peter Stevenson and many other characters. Since truckers seldom exchange names on the road because we all know the chances of running into each other again is at best remote, I have no idea who that driver is. If he's reading this, he'll know. Thanks, driver. And keep the sunny side up.

During the time I've been working on this book, I've had three different driver managers: Jason Frye, Ken White, and Jimmy Zoani. In my company the DM is the link between the driver and the company. Any of them could have said, "Either you drive or you write but not both." Instead, they were all very understanding when I needed time for this or that. Thanks, guys!

My friends and family deserve a big thanks, many of them telling me for years I should write a book someday. The day is here, and they've all continued to encourage me throughout. One of them, Lynn Leek, gave me many ideas and suggestions.

Henry "Hank" Hamilton in the story is in real life Hank Hilton, an old—and I do mean old—trucking buddy and a factual character in the story. I tried to keep it as realistic as possible and Hank helped me a lot in doing so. Even the way we met as depicted in the story is true. When finished I sent a copy to him and in typical form said, "Not bad for a old coot." Thanks, Hank!

Last but not least is another former camper from 21 years ago, Cindy Pawlicki, also a true character in the story with a changed name. Cindy is now a pharmacist in Phoenix. A few years ago while passing through, we met for breakfast. While eating she suggested I come up with a story about truckers. Completely lacking in ideas I asked, "Like what?" She suggested, "How about going into a ghost town to pick up a load?" It was just enough to spark my imagination, and the rest is history. Thanks, Cindy, and everybody else for your ideas, suggestions, help, and encouragement.

## INTRODUCTION

The big wheels roll all over this country on the interstate highways, U.S. and state routes delivering to us most of everything we eat, wear, play with, and use in one way or another. Without the big trucks, this country would not be what it is today.

Legend has it that cross-country truck drivers are a breed unto themselves, and I guess in some ways we are. Some stay on the road for two or three weeks, others as long as two or three months, and in a few cases, even longer. There are training teams, teams among friends, and husband and wife teams. And there's the solo driver. He or she is perceived as being the rugged independent individualist, the loner who has no need for people and is probably a little on the antisocial side. Individuals who lack social skills and have a problem dealing with people are at a definite disadvantage. The driver is constantly dealing with a variety of people—police, Department of Transportation (DOT) officers, shippers and consignees, dispatchers, driver managers (DMs). Every driver from time to time is late for an appointment, because of traffic, weather, or a breakdown. In such a situation, the company is supposed to notify the shipper or receiver, both known as the customer. However, sometimes it doesn't get done and the driver is left to deal with an irate customer, explain the situation, and smooth things over for the sake of the his company. At times like these, the driver must become a diplomat and deal with the situation in the most productive way possible.

Then there are the "four-wheelers," or cars. Although most of them are pretty good drivers, there are those few who make life interesting. For instance, I was once traveling through Wyoming on I-80 following a station wagon from New York. We were both traveling between 65 and 70 miles an hour with 200 to 300 feet between us when the driver suddenly slammed on his brakes, coming to a dead stop on the interstate so he could point out a herd of antelope to his children. I don't think anyone in the family had any idea how close they came to death that day.

Then there's the guy who is approaching his exit. A big truck is in the right-hand lane also approaching the same exit. Anyone with even a small amount of intelligence and common sense would pull behind the truck and wait until he gets to his exit. However, there are always a few, who in trying to save a second or two, zip around the truck then, taking his own life and the trucker's in his own hands, cuts directly in front of the truck. More often than not this is done without a signal. The trucker slams on his brakes to keep from killing someone. These kind of drivers think they made it but in reality, they didn't. The trucker gave it to them.

Then there are those who enter a 60- or 70-mile-an-hour lane on the interstate, moving at 40 mph or so with no signal or without using the mirrors. Again most of them make it but seem totally oblivious to what they've done to the traffic flow behind them. If the trucker cannot move into another lane at that time he will be forced to slow down by downshifting and applying the brakes. As a result it may take from a half to one mile to regain his cruising speed thus affecting all traffic behind him. Meanwhile the car that caused the problem is long gone. There would be far more accidents between four-wheelers and big trucks if the professional driver weren't constantly on the lookout for the idiot. Again these are only a few examples of hundreds I could use. Those of you who have never driven or ridden in a big truck may think I'm exaggerating, but those who have driven a truck for at least a week know I'm not.

We sit up high enough to see what's going on inside a lot of the cars, vans, and pickup trucks that pass us. It's amazing what people do while driving. Some of it can be quite distracting;

however, I'll keep it clean. One person passed me while working on his laptop, perhaps a proposal on the seat next to him that he was referring to while talking on a cell phone. Somehow I got the idea he wasn't paying too much attention to me. Then there was the woman who passed me while knitting—with both hands. Seeing people reading books, magazines, and newspapers is very common. I've had several young people pass sitting on the seat with their legs crossed, and one young lady passed with both feet out the side window. Cruise control is great; however, sometimes being able to get to the brake quickly isn't all that bad either. They cannot imagine what would have happened if a deer had run across the road in front of them.

Everybody on the road is constantly communicating with the people around him or her. If you have neither signal on, you're telling everyone you are going to continue going straight, staying in the lane you are now in. If you have your right signal on, you're telling everyone you're going to turn right or move into the right lane. If you have you're left signal on, you're telling everyone you're going to turn left or you're going to move into the left lane. I realize this is a difficult concept to grasp but I hope everyone is still with me. If you have neither signal on yet you turn one way or the other, you're a liar because you just told everybody you were going straight.

As I drive around the country, my unscientific observations find that on average, only about 25 percent of the people on the intestates use their signals, although it varies by state. New York and Wisconsin are the best at about 70 percent, while Texas, Arkansas, Louisiana, Mississippi, and Alabama are the worst at between 4 to 10 percent. Many people put their signals on after crossing the centerline but by that time it's too late. There's no need to tell me what you already did.

Some of you may be wondering what I've observed about my fellow truck drivers. Well, the average nationwide is about 80 percent, when I eliminate the five previously mentioned states. But if I were to include those five states, the national average goes down to about 60 percent, still way above the national average for four-wheelers.

I've also been observing the police officers around the country and have found that only about 23 percent of them use their signals. To this day, I still have not seen a police officer in Arkansas or Florida use their signal for any turn.

What about the professional driver? Do they all drive like professionals? I wish I could say yes, but I can't. Some drive too fast in potentially dangerous situations. Many tailgate and there's nothing more intimidating than looking in your rearview mirror while driving a smaller vehicle at 60 mph and seeing nothing but a monster grill.

Cross-country drivers go wherever the shipper or consignee happens to be and some of these places aren't easy to get to in a big truck. For those of you who have driven through downtown Manhattan and were ready to pull your hair out, put yourself in something that's 8½ feet wide, 75 feet long, and in two pieces. Or perhaps in rural areas, try following directions like these: turn right and drive down a small, winding country dead-end road for two miles. Only then you find out the person giving you the directions didn't know the difference between his right and left and really meant for you to take the dead-end road on your left. Remember, you can't pull into somebody's driveway and turn around. All you can do is back out and hope that when you finally get to your destination you don't run into the person who gave you the wrong directions. You don't want to be charged with murder. Or try crossing the Big Horn Mountains on U.S. 14 during a driving snowstorm, knowing that one little mistake and you could jackknife and go over the edge into nothingness. These are only a few of hundreds of examples drivers find themselves in every day.

The following is a story about a driver being dispatched to a most unlikely place and yet similar to situations many of us have found ourselves in. The characters in this story are fictitious. The town of Slippery Gulch is also fictitious; however, it's not unlike many ghost towns still found throughout the West. I sincerely hope you enjoy.

# ONE

Hi, folks. Jake here. Jake Winters. I'm a "long haul," or cross-country, truck driver; you know, the type of guy you four-wheelers love to hate but can't get along without. I understand. I drive around on four wheels on those rare occasions when I'm home. I had an experience earlier this year I thought you might find interesting.

In July, I picked up a load in Lincoln, Nebraska, going to Salt Lake City, Utah. I had just pulled out of the scales at Evanston, Wyoming, on I-80, when I noticed a large, black sedan tailgating me. Many drivers of both cars and trucks do this to reduce their wind resistance and increase their fuel mileage, forgetting how dangerous it is to both themselves and their passengers. I shake these people as soon as I can. I slowed to 45 miles per hour, but he didn't pass me. I then sped up to 70, but he stayed with me. I then got off on an exit and got back on again. But again he stayed with me. As I was approaching Parley Summit, I noticed a West truck coming up on me. West is a company that hauls both refrigerated and flatbed trailers.

I picked up the mike of my CB radio and made a call. "West, you got a copy on this westbound QZX?"

"Yeah, QZ, go ahead."

"Thanks for the comeback. I'd like you to do a favor for me. When you go by that black sedan, could you look at the license plate number and see if there's anything unusual about the occupants? This guy's been on my tail for 30 miles and I can't shake him no matter what I do."

"Be glad to, QZ," the West driver said. After a short time, he got back to me. "QZ, have you robbed any banks lately?"

"Not lately," I said with a chuckle. "Why?"

"That's a U.S. government car. Now, I could be wrong but if I were to take a guess, I'd say you've got a couple of feds on your tail."

"Thanks, you really know how to make a guy's day."

"My pleasure, QZ, and good luck."

I thanked him for his help again and he sped on.

I decided to pull into the area designated for big trucks to check their brakes before starting the 12-mile descent into Salt Lake from Parley Summit and find out what was going on. I set the brakes, turned off the truck and got out. Two men were already walking up the length of my 53-foot trailer to meet me.

Both were big, though just about everyone's big to me. I'm only about 5-foot-8 and weigh 138 to 140 pounds depending on how many drops of water are on me at any given time. The one man had to be 6-foot-5 and 250 pounds and had a nose that I'm sure had been broken more than once and not from playing football. He looked to be about 40 with a few gray hairs mixed in with his full head of light brown hair. He had a scar under his right eye, which made him look rather unfriendly.

He said in a deep baritone voice with a Northeastern accent, "Are you Mr. Jake Winters?"

I looked at him and said, "Who wants to know?"

"I'm Special Agent McCade, FBI," he said. Then the passenger introduced himself in a slightly higher and very Southern voice. "And I'm Special Agent Jones, FBI." Both produced identification.

Jones was not as large, perhaps 6 feet and roughly 180 pounds. He was about 35, blond diminishing hair, and blue eyes in a friendly face. He said, "We're investigating the possible hijacking of interstate freight en route from Montana to Nevada and believe a Jake Winters was the driver. Are you Jake Winters?"

"Yeah, I'm Jake Winters," I said hesitantly. "What can I do for you?"

McCade said, "We'd like to ask you a few questions."

"Okay, ask away. But to get the answers, you'll have to talk to my attorney." They didn't look too surprised with my response and finally said I was to drive to the terminal in Salt Lake and park it.

"No, I don't think so. I've got a load to deliver before going to the terminal," I said.

"Arrangements have already been made for that, Mister Winters. Just go straight to the terminal. We're to escort you to Butte, Montana," McCade said.

I stood there looking from one to the other and finally said, "You serious?"

"Very serious," McCade said. "We'll get into Butte sometime this afternoon where you'll meet with other agents and your attorney."

"Oh, then I guess we're not going by truck."

"Not hardly," McCade said. "There's a plane waiting for us at the Salt Lake City airport."

"Not that I don't believe you, but you do realize I'll have to contact my company before I do anything."

"That's fine but we do have to move quickly," Jones said.

I got back in the truck and sent a message to Jason, my driver manager, via the onboard satellite communication system, in other words, a computer, which allows instant communication between the driver and the company anytime and from any place. I explained to him where I was and what the FBI instructed me to do and asked for confirmation.

I got what I needed from Jason in seconds and was told to cooperate with the FBI 100 percent. I asked why I was the last to know about this and all he said was, "Orders from the FBI."

The agents were waiting outside my truck. After receiving my last message, I looked down at them and said, "When I get to the terminal, I'll have to drop the trailer, park my truck, and take the paperwork into the terminal then pack for the trip. How long should I plan for?"

"You may not be there that long, but I'd pack for a week if I were you," McCade said.

"Okay then, let's do it. Just don't tailgate me anymore. If I kicked up something off the road, it could go through your windshield." I pulled back onto I-80 and headed for the terminal in Salt Lake, the FBI in tow. I smiled to myself when I noticed they were no longer tailgating.

When I got to the terminal, I had to go through security to get to the truck parking area. Cars were not allowed in the truck parking area; however, the FBI was right behind me. I could have told them they can't follow me into the truck parking area, but I wanted to have a little fun. Besides I was kind of curious to see what security would do with a car full of FBI agents. Security won.

Meanwhile, I dropped the trailer, drove around to the truck parking area, and took my paperwork in. The agents were waiting for me along with Jason. I handed Jason my paperwork and asked about the status of my truck. Normally, if you're off the road longer than four or five days, you're asked to move out of your truck and turn it in. But under these circumstances, there would be no problem. As I walked out with the agents, Jason wished me luck.

## TWO

My problems began on June 29, 2001. I had been dispatched from St. Louis to Butte, Montana, with a load of paper. I had a 5:00 A.M. appointment and was empty by 5:15. Paper loads are usually a quick load and quick unload, which is nice. I emptied out on my onboard computer, meaning I'd sent my company the proper information to let them know I had completed that assignment and would soon be ready for my next one. We can get such information as the name, address, phone number, contact person, and directions for both the shipper and consignee. If directions are not available, we can add them for the next driver once we get them. We can send information to the company about mechanical problems we're having (including total breakdowns), let them know where we are, and get help without ever leaving the truck. At the same time, the company can see where we are within 50 feet at any time. This is useful if it's a time-sensitive load and the consignee wants to know where we are. Since this is an expensive procedure, it's not often used.

I got back on the computer to let my driver manager know I was going to the truck stop nearby for a shower and breakfast and would be ready for my next load at 6:30. Just as I got back to my truck, full and refreshed, information for my next assignment was coming in. This information usually includes name, address, phone number, and contact person for the shipper and consignee. It also includes fuel stops and their exact locations, recommended routing, and both loaded miles (how far it is from the shipper to the consignee) and deadhead miles (how far it is from where I am to the shipper.)

I was to pick up a load at J and J Mines on Blood Run Road, Slippery Gulch, Montana. I love going into little towns around America. I think they're far more interesting than the larger cities, and the driving is usually much easier. You don't have the traffic to contend with.

My contact at the mine was Jeremiah Peabody. I looked in my atlas under the Montana glossary for the town of Slippery Gulch but it wasn't listed. The deadhead miles to the shipper were not listed, so I hoped that meant Slippery Gulch was a little burg that had been incorporated into the city of Butte years ago. I asked the computer for directions to the shipper, but after a few minutes it said, "No directions available." Since no phone number was listed in the original information pertaining to the shipper, I asked for the number. After a couple of minutes the computer said, "No phone number available."

Now I had a problem. I had to pick up a load in a town that was not listed in the state glossary. I had no directions and no phone number. I went to the fuel desk in the truck stop and talked to Jack, at least that was the name on his name tag. Jack was a pimple-faced 20-year-old. He had bright orange hair on the right and purple on the left. He had multiple pieces of steel piercing each ear, two in his right nostril, and several in his left eyebrow. He also had a chunk sticking through his tongue. Forgive me, but the only word that came to my mind was "freak." I said with a great deal of sympathy, "Oh man, did you have the staple gun facing in the wrong direction?" He looked up and I found myself looking into a set of bloodshot eyes. I figured he was on a little more than just pink lemonade. He didn't say a word. I went on to my next question. "Do you know where the town of Slippery Gulch is?"

He said, "Never heard of it." Well, at least he could talk but I decided I wasn't going to get any more information from him, so I thanked him for his help—if that's what you call it—and called the State Highway Patrol.

I explained to the person who answered that I was a truck driver, and I was to pick up a load at J and J Mines in Slippery Gulch, Montana. I explained that although I had the address and contact person at the mines, I did not have directions or a phone number and could not find Slippery Gulch listed in the state glossary. I asked if he had any idea where it was.

He said, "It sounds familiar, but I don't know where it is. There're so many ghost towns in this part of Montana, it's hard to keep track of all of them. Why don't you try the county sheriff. If they can't help, call back and I'll try something else."

"I don't think it's a ghost town. Why would I be dispatched to it for a load if it was?"

"Good question. Are you sure you have the right name?"

"Yeah, I'm sure."

"Give the sheriff a try. As I said, he may be able to help."

I thanked him for his help, hung up and dialed the sheriff. I explained who I was, my situation, and asked him if he knew where the town was.

"I've heard of it. It's a ghost town up in Jefferson County near Basin, but I don't know how to get to it. Why are they sending you to a ghost town?"

"Are you sure it's a ghost town?" I asked.

"Well, it was. If I were you, I'd call my company, explain the situation, and make sure they're giving you the correct information. Why don't you call them first, then give me a call back."

"Okay," I said. "I'll call you back in a few minutes."

I called Jason, my driver manager, explained the situation, and asked if I could talk to the load planner for Montana. I was put on hold for a couple of minutes. I again explained the situation and said I wanted a verbal confirmation on this load before I went driving into the mountains bound for a ghost town. I heard the computer keys in the background and finally the load planner said, "We received a phone call from a Mr. Jeremiah Peabody, the owner of the J and J Mines. He asked to have a truck sent in on June 29, 2001, between 10:00 A.M. and 12:00 to pick up a load to be shipped to Smith and Associates in Reno, Nevada. No appointment time set."

"Well, okay." I sighed. "I will keep Jason posted." I thanked him and hung up.

I called the sheriff's dispatcher and explained to him exactly what the load planner had said. He said, "Okay then, I'd like you to call Sheriff Livingston. He's the sheriff of Jefferson County. I just talked to him so he's expecting your call. He doesn't know exactly how to get there either, but he knows an individual in Basin who can direct you."

He gave me the phone number; I thanked him for his help, and hung up. Then I called Sheriff Livingston. The sheriff had a deep baritone voice and sounded like he might be huge. I explained I had just talked to the load planner and he confirmed verbally the information I had on the load plus a little more.

"Okay," he said. "All I know is you have to go to Basin first. A guy by the name of George Swansen, who owns the Silver Dollar Saloon in Basin, is more knowledgeable about the ghost mines and towns near Basin than anyone I know. I'm sure he can help you. Here's his phone number."

I thanked him for his help and called George. I once again went through my entire story. George listened without interruption. When I was finished, he asked, "Do you know how to get to Basin?"

"Yes," I said. "I see it on the map."

"Okay. When you get off I-15 at the Basin exit, go under the interstate, turn left and go back into town. I'm on the left side of the road. Just park in front of the saloon."

"My rig is 75 feet long. Will there be room?"

"In Basin, don't worry about it."

"Okay, I'll leave right away."

"I'll be here." The receiver clicked. I could not get a read on Mr. Swansen. He'd been short and impersonal. I chalked it up to being a Swede. I started "The Babes," my affectionate nickname for my truck, and headed for Basin.

The drive to Basin from Butte was beautiful. At first, you see the Pintler Mountains. They were still wearing a little snow up there. Within 4 or 5 miles I drove into the Deer Lodge National Forest. From that point on, I drove through valleys and canyons, all deep in the lush forest.

As I was approaching the Basin exit, I looked to my left and saw a few small buildings that looked to be on the outskirts of town. However, as I passed under the interstate and turned left, I realized those few buildings were not the outskirts of Basin, they were Basin. I'd take Basin over New York City, any time.

I drove down the main street, the only street going through town, looking for the Silver Dollar Saloon. I spotted it up ahead, pulled to the left side of the road and parked. George was right, there was plenty of room. I set the air brakes, turned The Babes off, stepped out, and was immediately hit by the peace and quiet of the place. I was a long way from Broadway.

# THREE

I started to walk toward the saloon when the door opened and a large man walked out. I guess he heard the air breaks. "Mr. Swansen?" I asked.

"No, I'm George," he said with a big smile. "Mr. Swansen is my father." We shook hands.

George was about forty, perhaps 6-foot-3 and in the range of 240 pounds, with broad shoulders and a large neck. His brown hair showed gray and his blue eyes were friendly. He had an easy smile. I liked him at once.

George took one look at my long nose Freightliner and 53-foot trailer and said slowly, "Oh, my God. You're going to drive that thing into Slippery Gulch?" At this point that was not a question I needed to hear.

"Obviously you know something I don't," I said.

"This is not going to be the easiest drive you've ever made by a long shot, but let's go in for a cup of coffee before you leave."

The saloon was long and narrow with a long bar and a large mirror behind it. There were a few tables in the room. All were empty. Being 8:00 A.M. we had the place to ourselves.

George walked behind the bar and said, "How do you take it?"

"Just sugar will be fine."

A few silent moments later he handed me a coffee and said, "Look, I've been thinking about this. Is there someone you could call to verbally verify this load?"

"I'm way ahead of you; I already did. I talked to both my driver manager and the load planner for Montana. An individual called the company two days ago requesting a truck to come

14

into J and J Mines between 10:00 and 12:00 this morning and pick up a load going to Reno, Nevada. The address was simply Blood Run Road, Slippery Gulch, Montana."

"Who made the phone call?"

"A guy by the name of Jeremiah Peabody."

"I didn't know the mine up there is called J and J Mines, but I have heard of a Jeremiah Peabody. I just don't remember where and I don't think I've ever met him. The mine shut down around 1900 and I hadn't heard of it reopening, but I don't know everything that's going on around here. The town was abandoned early in the century. Any idea what kind of load you're picking up?"

"No idea. What kind of a mine is it?"

"It was a copper mine." He emphasized the word was.

"Well, I suppose I'd be picking up copper then."

He came around the bar, coffee in hand, and perched on the stool two down from mine. He talked to me in the mirror. "You don't know much about copper mining, do you?"

"Well, to be perfectly honest, I don't know a thing about it."

"The copper when mined is the raw material. It is put into what is called a crusher and ground to almost a powder form. It is shipped to a smelter where it is melted and formed into ingots. Then it is shipped in that form to foundries around the country or sometimes to other countries." He turned to look directly at me. "I guarantee you, you're not picking up copper."

"What else could I be picking up?"

"That's the question of the hour. I have no idea. When you come back through Basin, would you mind stopping in and letting me know?"

"Sure, no problem. By the way, any idea as to how the road got its name?"

"Blood Run Road? Interesting name, isn't it? From what I understand, back in the 1800s there were so many gunfights on Main Street the—quote—'decent people of the town' started to complain. So the town council got together and passed a law stating there could be no more gunfights on Main Street. If you wanted to blow somebody's brains out, you had to do it on the side street. Supposedly so much blood had run down the road it became known as Blood Run Road. I don't know if there's any truth to it but it sounds good, doesn't it?"

"Yeah, it sure does. Now, how do I get there?"

"You can just back up a couple 100 feet then turn right onto Basin Creek Road. You go for 4 or 5 miles, turn right onto the third road on the right. Go for about 6 miles and crest a hill. Go down the hill for about a half mile and at the bottom you'll be in Slippery Gulch."

"Sounds nice and easy. Am I in for any surprises?"

"Where would you like me to start?"

"How about from the time I turn on Basin Creek Road."

"Well, to begin with, I'll find someone to give you an escort to the third road. The first two roads you're likely to miss. They're really hard to see. If you miss one or both and turn on what you think is the third road, you're going to end up in big trouble. After driving for 6 or 8 miles, you'll come to a washed-out road and have to back out and I guarantee you, you don't want to do that." He thought for a minute. "Let me call my brother-in-law. I'll see if he has time."

Although I could only hear half of the conversation, it wasn't too difficult to figure out what was being said on the other end. "Mike, this is George. You got about a half hour to spare? Well, I have a truck driver here who has to get into Slippery Gulch. Yeah, Slippery Gulch…No, I'm not kidding…An 18-wheeler…I don't know. Wait, I'll ask." At that point he turned to me and asked, "How long is your trailer?"

"It's 53 feet."

He repeated what I'd said into the phone. There was a short pause. "Yeah, that's the same thing I said when I first saw it. Well, if there's someone up there, the road must be open. He says someone called his company and asked them to send in a truck to pick up a load. I don't think someone would request a truck if they knew the road was closed…Somebody by the name of Jeremiah Peabody…Yeah, the name sounds familiar to me too, but I can't place him…Okay, see you in a few."

"My brother-in-law will be here in a few minutes. He'll get you to the right road."

"Once I make that turn, what do I have to look forward to?"

"Once you leave Basin, you'll be climbing almost steadily until you start your descent into Slippery Gulch. It's a pretty steep climb most of the way, but at least the road is dry. Haven't had any snow since April and no rain in a month. There are some tight curves—you'll take up the whole road and then some going around them; but of course, you'll take up most of the road anyway. There's no way you're going to be able to keep your trailer wheels on the road going around most of those curves. But don't worry about going into ditches or over cliffs. There's only 200 yards where you go along a cliff, but it's straight. Just don't look down and you'll be okay. About a quarter of a mile past there you'll start down into town. Make sure you've got your air built up to the max 'cause you're going to need it. It's not long but it's steep."

"How long do you think this little drive is going to take me?"

"Although it's no more than 6 or 7 miles, I'd guess between 1½ to 2 hours."

George went to pour both of us more coffee. I said, "So the road is dry…meaning, I shouldn't lose traction?"

"You shouldn't as long as you take it easy. If you stop half-way up a hill and then gun it, you're going to have a problem but if you keep it at a nice, steady, slow speed, you'll do okay."

"So I shouldn't have a problem," I said with growing doubt.

"If you use your intelligence and common sense, you'll do fine. Don't get me wrong: You're not going to have it easy. How long have you been driving?"

"About 10 years."

"Good. You'll do okay. Sure glad I don't have to do it though. Of course, since I've never driven a big truck before, driving down I-15 would be a challenge for me." At that we both laughed. Mine was a little strained.

Just then a beautiful, blond-haired woman walked in; she was trailed by a man. The man said, "George, you feeding him some of your world-famous bull?"

"No, not me." George introduced me to his brother-in-law. Mike Dowdy appeared to be in his late thirties. He was about 5-foot-10, 180 pounds, and had brown eyes and dark brown hair well over his ears. He wore a red plaid shirt, jeans, and well-worn work boots. He looked like he just came in from checking his trapline. His firm handshake showed confidence. George then introduced me to his sister, Jane. She was about 35, had long blond hair, blue eyes, and was petite but very well endowed. (Who cares about anything else?) She also displayed a lot of confidence in her handshake.

I said, "You know, when I heard George had a sister, I was afraid you might look like George. But I assure you, you don't." Mike and Jane just about rolled in laughter. George sent me a look that could have killed, but with a good-humored twinkle in his eye, then started laughing himself. Mike came over, shook my hand again, and said, "I like you already."

George said to me, "You know, stranger, if you weren't so damned old, I'd shoot an insult right back at you."

All I could do was give a laugh, which relaxed my mounting tension over the drive ahead. I felt like the four of us had been friends before, somewhere.

George asked, "How about a cup of coffee you two?"

"You buying?" Jane asked.

"Of course."

"Well this is a first. Sure, why not?" Mike kidded.

"No more for me," I said. "If I have any more, it will take me twice as long to get there because I'll have to stop every 5 minutes to get rid of it."

Jane asked, "Where are you from?"

"I live in the Buffalo, New York, area."

"Gee. You're a long ways from home," Jane said. "You get home often?"

"I go home every two or three months."

"Wow, that's not very often. Are you married?" Jane asked.

"Nope. Came within two weeks once but it didn't work out."

"Oh, I'm sorry to hear that," Jane said.

"Hey, don't worry about it. I'm an old, independent cuss. I just wasn't ready to settle down, and I don't think she was either."

"Then I guess it worked out for the best for both of you?"

"Oh, I don't think there's any doubt about it."

"What does QZX stand for?" Mike asked.

"The founder and owner of the company is Quincey Zeller, thus the QZ. The X stands for Xpress."

"Have you been driving a truck all these years?" Mike asked.

"No, I used to be a school teacher."

"You're kidding!" George asked. "You gave up teaching to drive a truck?"

"Well, I got tired of kids and lost my patience. I also got tired of parents, other teachers, and administrators. I got tired of getting in the car every morning and driving over the same roads to get to the same four walls every day. And then driving over the same roads to get home every night. In other words, I burned out. When I was a kid, I wanted to do two things when I grew up. I wanted to be a teacher and I wanted to drive a big truck. I finally realized it was time to make the change. The rest is history. It does have its advantages: My truck doesn't talk back, it doesn't have parents, and it can't sue me."

They all laughed. "You must be the most highly educated truck driver on the road," Jane said.

"I know the stereotype truck driver is basically a first-grade dropout, and some of them may sound like it, but in reality, that just isn't the case. Most are high school graduates, and there are more college graduates than ever driving big rigs, some with master's and doctorate degrees. And they're all driving for basically the same reason I am. They got tired of doing the same thing, in the same place, in the same way, day in and day out; they wanted to experience the freedom and independence of the open road.

"Well, I'll be," Jane said. "Don't you ever get lonely?"

"Never. I like people and I'm always meeting new and interesting people every place I go. However, I also enjoy my solitude. I'm an avid reader. And I've also been blessed with a lot of very good friends back home."

"So what are you going to do next?" Jane asked.

"Oh, I don't know. Maybe retire, buy a camper and drive around the country."

"Nothing like something different." Jane said.

"Well, I know it sounds about the same, but then I'll be able to go where and when I want to and stay as long as I want."

# FOUR

Shifting gears, Mike asked, "So Jeremiah Peabody is the one who called your company?"

"Yes, and he's also my contact person once I get to the mine."

"I wish I could remember where I've heard that name before," Mike said. "I was up there about 2 years ago. I know he wasn't there then and I'm sure I've never met him before."

"Yeah, I feel the same way," George said. "When you were up there, was anybody there?"

"No, nobody. I had the place to myself," Mike said. "It looked as if nobody had been there for decades, except for—" He looked away to a distant place on his left and said, "Oh never mind. You'll think I'm nuts."

Jane, looking a little concerned, said, "No we won't. Go ahead, Mike. What happened?"

Hesitantly he said, "I walked around town. It's kind of interesting you know, a fairly good-sized ghost town that time and people have completely forgotten. I've walked around the town before, but this time it felt different."

"Felt different?" George asked. "What do you mean?"

"Well, you know how sometimes you're alone—you know for a fact you're alone—yet you feel as if someone else is there?" I nodded my head, but without conviction. "Well, that's the way I felt that day. Not only that, I felt I was being watched. This is where you're going to think I'm nuts."

"We already know that. Go ahead," George said, reaching a long arm to pat Mike's shoulder.

"Well, I was walking between these two buildings, you know, down a little alley, when I came across some tracks. Fresh tracks."

"So. The town's in the mountains," Jane said.

During this whole time I sat there not saying a word. I felt certain they were trying to psych me out, going into a ghost town and all. I decided I wasn't going to fall for it, so I'd play along for now.

"They weren't animal tracks, Jane. They were human, and they were small. They belonged to a child."

"Could they have been a woman's?" George asked.

"No. I'm a good enough tracker to tell the difference. They were definitely a child's, a boy's."

"Yeah, that's true," George said. "How could you tell it was a boy though?"

"Boys run different!"

"Now you sound like a sexist," Jane said smiling.

"I am. You know that," Mike said smiling back.

"So who was it and what was he doing up there?" George continued.

"I don't have an answer to either question. I said I came across the tracks and that's just what happened. They just started there between the buildings. There wasn't a door or window in either building. They just started. I followed them to the end of the alley and they stopped as suddenly as they had started."

"Wait a minute," Jane said. "Things don't work that way."

"Couldn't he have jumped to the boardwalk on either side of the alley?" George asked.

"No. He was running and he didn't stop at the end of the alley, just his tracks did! And there was no push-off, which you would have seen if he had jumped one way or the other."

"So what did you do?" George asked.

"I'll tell you what I did. I got the hell out of there and I haven't been back since."

We all sat there for a few minutes until I broke the silence. "George, you were telling me a little while ago that you've been there before. Have you ever experienced anything like that?"

"Nothing like that. But I have to admit, while walking around, I had the feeling I was being watched. Alone, in a place like that, your imagination can get the best of you. I figured that's what it was and left it at that."

"That's what I thought it was. But when I saw the prints, well, that changed everything," Mike added.

We all sat quietly again, deep in our own thoughts. I wanted to say, "Hey, Mike, time to cut the bull," but I didn't. I didn't know these people well. I decided to play it out and see what happened.

George finally spoke up. "Mike, do you think Jake will be okay up there?"

"Oh, I don't think he'll have a problem. Obviously there are a few people up there working now and they're going to be expecting him. Jake, any idea what you're picking up?"

"I had assumed I was going to pick up a load of copper since I'm going to a copper mine but George set me straight on that. I don't know the first thing about mining. If I'm not picking up copper though, what could I be picking up?"

The three of them looked at each other and finally George said, "I really don't know."

Mike said, "Maybe some kind of equipment."

"What kind of equipment?" Jane asked.

"Well, I don't know," Mike stated. "But if they're closing the mine, maybe they're selling some equipment to minimize the loss."

"Mike, that mine closed 100 years ago," George said. "The time to sell equipment would have been then. Who in their right mind is going to buy 100-year-old mining equipment?"

"What about a museum?" Jane asked.

"Now that's a thought," Mike said. "Where is the load going?"

"To a business called Smith and Associates in Reno, Nevada," I said.

"When a museum buys equipment, it doesn't go through a middleman if it doesn't have to," Jane said.

"Maybe this Smith and Associates is a company that restores machinery for museums," Mike said.

"Yes, I suppose that could be the case," Jane signed.

"Hey, guys, I hate to break up this line of thought but I really think I'd better get moving."

"Good point," George said." If you leave now you should be there between 9:30 and 10:00. If you have a chance, take a minute to walk around. It's really kind of neat."

"Yeah, I'd really like to do that. By the way, I may be small but I really don't scare too easily."

They all looked at each other in puzzlement for a moment.

I went on, "Mike, I really enjoyed your story but I've been telling stories like that for years. I think they're great, but they don't really bother me."

"Wait a minute. You think I made up that story about the footprints?"

"Hey, it's a great story."

"Jake, I'm kind of embarrassed to tell you this, but I don't have the kind of imagination to make up a story like that. It really happened and it spooked the hell out of me."

"Okay, I'll keep an eye out for small footprints."

"You don't really believe me, do you?"

"To tell you the truth, Mike, in watching your eyes and listening to your voice, I can't say it's false. But you have to understand, it's a hard story to believe."

"He's right, Mike," Jane said. "It doesn't make sense."

Mike thought for a minute and then said, "Yeah, it is hard to believe. I guess that's why I never mentioned it before. I knew no one would ever believe me, and I don't blame you but I swear to God, it really happened."

At this point, I had no choice; I had to believe him. A little chill ran down my spine as I decided it was time to go.

I rose and started for the door. The four of us left the building and walked to my tractor. When we got out there George was saying, "You know, I've been thinking. Do you have a cell phone in there?"

"Yeah, I do."

"Good. When you get to the turnoff, give me a call. When you get about 2 miles down the road, call again, and then when you get to the town, try again. I don't know if it will work from there but we can give it a try. Now also, it will take you about an hour and a half or so to get from here to there. Let's figure 2 hours in, 1 hour to look, 2 hours to load, and 2 hours to get back to Basin. That's 7 hours. If we lose contact or if you're not back here by 6:00 or so, we'll come looking for you."

"Sounds good. I really appreciate your concern and interest but I really don't expect to have any major problems."

"I don't think you will either, but let's face it, it's not like you're driving to Butte. It's better to be prepared."

"I agree." At that point I thanked them all again, shook hands, turned, and climbed up into the truck.

"This sure is a beautiful truck," Mike said. "Would you mind if I climbed up in there for a minute? I've never been in one of these."

"Come on up," I said moving over to make room. As he moved onto the air ride seat, the first thing he looked at was the gearshift.

"What's this?" he asked. "This isn't the gearshift, is it?"

"Yes it is."

"Is this an automatic?"

"Yep, it sure is."

"I didn't know they made automatics for big trucks."

"Well, to be perfectly honest, until I got this truck, I didn't either. I've got to clutch it when I first start out and again when I come to a complete stop. Other than that, I just sit back and watch the scenery go by. It upshifts and downshifts and I just sit there and decide when to put the brake on and steer. It's great!"

Mike looked down at George and said, "George, you should see this thing. It's really something."

"George, Jane, come on up and look around if you'd like."

They both climbed up. While the men were most interested in the dashboard, Jane was more impressed with the sleeper berth, storage space, and double bunks. Both George and Mike asked questions about the different knobs, switches, buttons, and gauges. As they climbed down, the men asked to see the engine. After answering several more questions, I finally had to admit I was a mechanical neophyte. If something happened that required more than checking the oil, water level, or air pressure in the tires, I was in trouble. However, I explained the computer and how our breakdown system worked. They were impressed.

Mike finally said, "Well, what do you think?"

"Yeah, it's time. Let's get moving." I closed the hood, climbed back into the cab, cranked The Babes over, and got ready for what I was wondering might turn out to be an adventure of a lifetime.

"Jake, do you have your CB radio on 19?"

"Yeah," I answered.

"Good. You ready?"

"All set. Let's do it!"

## FIVE

I pulled out, went to the end of town and found a place to turn around, came back, and made a left on Basin Creek Road, waving to George and Jane as I went by. I fell in behind Mike and started climbing almost at once. The woods of the Deer Lodge National Forest engulfed us within 300 yards of the post office.

We talked back and forth on the radio after leaving Basin and finally Mike said, "The first road is coming up in about 200 feet."

I picked up the mike and said, "Where?"

"You're just coming up on it now."

I looked over and just barely caught it buried in the trees. I would never have seen it if Mike hadn't pointed it out. The second road was the same. I picked up the mike and said, "Mike, if the next road is as tight as the last two, I'll never make the turn."

"It's tight but not as tight as the last two. You'll have to swing wide but you'll make it."

"How can I swing wide? I'm taking up darn near the whole road now."

"When I get to the turnoff, I'll stop. Walk up to the road and take a look but I'm sure you can make it."

"Okay," I said, but I was worried. People who have never driven a big truck are constantly overestimating the maneuverability of these big rigs and underestimating their length and width.

About another half mile and Mike came to a stop. I stopped, set the brakes, and walked up to him. When I got there he said, "Now do you see why George wanted me to escort you to this point?"

"Yeah, I sure do. Had I missed one or both of those roads, which I'm sure I would have, I'd be in big trouble."

"That's an understatement. Let's take a look at this turn and see what you think."

We walked up to the corner, if you could call it that. It was tight but Mike was right, it wasn't as bad as the last two. There was maybe 3 or 4 feet to pull off on the left and on the right, the trees didn't come right to the edge of the road the way they did at the last two corners.

"Well, what do you think?"

"This is going to be real tight, but I've got a chance if I slide the tandems all the way forward."

"Slide the tandems all the way forward! What do you mean?"

"Come back to the trailer and I'll show you. I may need your help anyway."

We walked back and I had him look under the trailer and just above the tires. I pointed out a track with a lot of holes in it. The same track is on the other side of the trailer. The two axles and eight wheels of the trailer slide forward and backward on that track. Four pins attached to the frame fit into the holes thus securing the wheels in place. By pulling a certain lever—I pointed to the handle—the pins come out of the holes so the wheels can slide. By setting just the trailer brakes, then putting the tractor in reverse or forward, you can slide the tandems. By sliding the tandems all the way forward you shorten the wheelbase of a 53-footer by a good ten feet, making it easier to make a sharp turn.

I explained all this to him as best I could and said, "If I can't get this lever out, I'll need your help." However, it came right out and locked. I went back to the tractor and set the trailer brakes, released the tractor brakes, and put it in reverse. As I backed the tractor up, instead of the wheels turning, they stayed put and slid forward to the front of the track, shortening the wheelbase. I set the tractor brakes, walked to the trailer tires, released the lever so the pins slammed back into the holes, and locked the slide. I was ready to go.

"I'll be," Mike said. "I didn't know you could do that."

"Well, I guess we both learned something today."

I climbed back into the cab and backed up about 200 feet, shifted into second, and crept forward keeping as far to the left as I could go. I started my turn into the road. At barely a creep, with Mike's help, I took a couple of branches off a tree and put a few scratches on the trailer but made it. I set the brakes and got out to thank Mike for everything.

"Hey, no problem. You've got a straight shot into town from here. Well it's anything but straight, but no curves worse than what you've already hit. What I mean is, there are no turnoffs. You'll still be climbing, but not as bad as the climb between Basin and here. You'll run next to that cliff for about 200 yards, but just don't look down and you'll be okay. Once you get past the cliff, you'll start your descent into town. It's about a 10 to 12 percent grade, so don't let it get away from you. There's a curve about halfway down but nothing major. The hill is about a half-mile long. Once you get into town, the first intersection you come to—in fact, the only intersection you'll come to—is Blood Run Road. You'd turn left to get to the mine, but if I were you, I'd walk up to the mine first and look around. I don't think there'll be enough room for you to turn around up there. You'll probably have to back into, it but check it out first. It's about a quarter of a mile. One curve but nothing major though it is fairly steep." At that he stuck out his hand and said, "Good luck."

There was something ominous in those words. I shook his hand and said, "Thanks. Hey, do you think I'm crazy for doing this?"

He hesitated for a minute. He may have been trying to figure out a way to answer me without causing me fear or suggesting I'm crazy. "Well, let's put it this way. Better you than me."

I called George to let him know where I was and tell him I'd try him from town, once I get there. The phone was working fine. So far, it had taken me 30 minutes. Hopefully, I was half-way there. I thanked Mike again and headed for the truck. He said, "Be careful and watch out for little footprints."

I chuckled and said, "Yeah, I'll do that. Hopefully I'll see you in a few hours," and I was off.

## SIX

The trip was uneventful until I got to the cliff, where I stopped and looked out my cab window. Apparently, there had been a landslide there long before Slippery Gulch was founded, then they cut the road across it. When the land moved, it slid down the hill to where the road is now and then off into nothingness. The road up had been narrow all the way along, but for these 200 yards it narrowed even more. To the right of the road, there was nothing. I set the brakes, climbed out, and walked up a ways. This was not pretty. The road was not much wider than the width of my truck. Beyond that was close to a sheer cliff, a 100 feet to the bottom. If the road couldn't hold the weight of my truck, we'd both be over the side. In that event I wouldn't have to worry about explaining to the company the loss of the truck.

I walked back, climbed aboard, and put her in first gear, better known to truckers as creeper gear. I moved forward, keeping to the left as far as I could just to keep the right side of the truck on the road. I said a little prayer, praying that in 3 minutes I'd still be moving forward and not sideways and down. Slowly I crept into what I referred to as the "dead zone," that portion of the road running next to the cliff. I was happy to be on the far side of the truck cab from the cliff. Then I realized that on the way back, I wouldn't be. I looked in the right mirror just in time to see a few rocks disappear into the void and held my breath. The tires were right on the edge. That 200 yards seemed like 200 miles, but like everything else, it also passed under my eighteen wheels and I was finally across. Now, on to Slippery Gulch.

A short time later I crested the hill. There, far below me and to the right, I got my first sight of Slippery Gulch. Mike was right, this was one steep slope. I set the brakes and got out of my cab for a better look. It was as if I was standing on the edge of the twilight zone. The town was a good 500 feet below me nestled in a deep valley surrounded by a thick, forbidding forest of conifers. The town itself was composed of 40 to 50 building of a variety of shapes and sizes, all of them colorless. It was as if I'd just gone through a time warp and been transported back to the 1800s. From this vantage point the town appeared to be motionless and dead. I thought I caught a small movement but looking more closely, there was nothing there. A shiver went down my spine. I thought about Mike's phantom footprints and realized I was letting my imagination get the best of me. At least I wouldn't be alone. Thank God for that.

Well, no time like the present. I climbed back in the cab and slowly started down. Just a little too fast on that dirt and I could go into a slide and a jackknife.

About halfway down the hill I was navigating a curve to the right when I spotted the mine to my left, high above the town. I could see no form of life. Where was everybody? A chill ran down my spine as I once again thought of the small footprints. My thoughts were running wild. What would I do if I ran across those small footprints coming from nowhere and going nowhere? The main thing now was to control my imagination. Sometimes that was easier said than done. No matter what happened, I was confident this was going to be an experience I'd be talking about for years, assuming I lived through it. I had to admit to myself, though, it sure beat New York City.

I pulled up close to the intersection of Main and Blood Run Road, stopped, set the air brakes, and turned off the engine. It was time to get out and wander for a bit before I walked the road to the mine to see what else I was in for. I thought about moving the truck to the side of the road, but it didn't look as if I'd be blocking an awful lot of traffic, so I left it there.

I got out of the truck but didn't lock it. I figured I had the town to myself, or at least that's the way it looked. I just stood there for a minute looking in different directions. This was a town perfectly preserved in time. I'd never been there before yet I recognized it. It was any number of towns I'd seen in the old Westerns from the 1940s and 1950s. It was as if Matt Dillon or Wyatt Earp would appear any moment. I had to admit this was spookier than what I had expected. Of course, Mike's story wasn't helping any.

To the left of my truck was the school and next to that was the church with a small playground in between. A wooden merry-go-round and a maypole were the only toys to be seen. I hadn't seen a maypole since my own childhood. I walked over to them expecting to see the small tracks of children in the dirt but there were none. Of course, this was late June and school would have been out of session for weeks. Then again maybe there were no children left in the town since the mine was once again closing.

I heard music and moved toward its source. On the other side of the street was a building that appeared to be a saloon. Next to the saloon was a building with a sign above the door that was barely readable. Jacob's Mercantile. The music sounded like an old player piano. As I got closer, I could hear people laughing and talking. Suddenly a man appeared out of nowhere. Obviously, I was looking toward the saloon and didn't notice him approach. He was a grizzly character, probably late 60s or early 70s, long, dirty, gray-haired, and with a long dirty beard. He was no more than 5-foot-4 or 5-foot-5, slight of build with rounded shoulders and a slight slump. His clothing was torn and dusty. He looked as if he'd just returned from World War II—from the losing side. Not only that, he smelled like it.

He squinted up at me and said, "You teamsters are all alike. Think ya own the damn road! Drive anywhere ya want! Park anywhere ya want! Well, go ahead, just park your rig in the middle of the road. See if I care! And that's the dumbest team of old nags I ever seen. What's wrong, don't they pay ya enough to get a good team?" With that he spit a stream of tobacco juice dangerously close to my right foot and walked off, muttering incoherently to himself.

I turned toward my truck to see if by chance someone was behind me, but of course there wasn't. What was he talking about, and what did he mean by "old nags"? Was that his attempt at humor? Or was he just a senile old man, seeing things?

I didn't have time to think about it. There was this old-fashioned music coming from the building that absorbed my attention more than the old man. I turned back to that building and continued my walk toward the saloon.

I decided to enter it to have a look around when suddenly a child began yelling. I turned around in time to see a screaming little boy run out from an alleyway toward me but looking behind him. He couldn't have been more than 4 years old. He ran right into me and then fell over. He was a cute kid, I think, but only the Lord knows how many thick layers of dirt coated his small face. He had blue eyes and long, blond hair, all filthy and matted. The right leg of his jeans was torn off just above the knee and the left one had a huge hole in the knee. The left sleeve of his shirt was gone at the shoulder, the right at the elbow. All the buttons of his shirt were missing. As he lay there on the ground, his protruding ribs said he hadn't had a good meal in months. Every part of his exposed skin was filthy. His feet were bare, leaving small tracks in the dirt. He appeared to be dazed. I knelt down next to him and asked if he was okay.

"Yeah, I'm okay."

"Who were you running from?"

"My old man. He's drunk and he was going to beat me, but I think he'll leave me alone now that you're here."

I offered him my hand to help him up but when I did, he cowered away from it with fear in his eyes. When he stood, he backed up two steps. His pants were held up by a piece of bailing twine. They barely hung on his small hips. He was no more than three feet tall and if he weighed forty pounds, he weighted a lot. Then I noticed he was missing his two front teeth. Four is too young to loose them naturally. I wondered if they'd been knocked out. I looked down the alley but saw no one. The boy was trembling. I asked, "Are you sure you're okay?"

Not sure whether to turn and bolt or stand his ground, he said, "Yeah, I'm sure."

"What's your name?"

"Peter Stevenson. What's yours?"

"Jake Winters. Does your dad beat you often?"

"Only when he can catch me."

"Where's your mom?"

"She died when I was born."

"Oh, I'm sorry to hear that." I had no idea how much of this was true especially since there was no one else in the alley. He was calming down so I decided to let it pass. "How many people live here?"

"Not many now. They're closing down the mine. What are you doing here?"

"I'm picking up a load at the mine."

With that his eyes widened and he said, "Stay away from old man Peabody. Is that your wagon? He's real mean. "

"He is?"

"Yeah. He's real mean to my dad. My dad say's he's going to get even someday. When he's mean to my dad, my dad's real mean to me. I can always tell when old man Peabody is mean to my dad."

"How can you do that?"

"Because, when he's mean to my dad, that's when dad beats me the worst."

At that I looked at the boy for signs of physical abuse but saw none; however, signs of neglect were everywhere. I decided to mention it to my three newfound friends when I got back to Basin. Maybe they could get someone in here to help him out. The thought of Basin recalled the strange tracks. I looked at the boy's feet and followed the small tracks he'd just made. My eyes moved up the alley until I could no longer see them from where I was standing. They started someplace and ended by me. No little boy can stand still for long, and neither could Peter. He moved around as we talked and his tracks danced around with him. Whatever tracks Mike thought he'd seen obviously didn't belong to this kid. I got an idea. I'd forgotten to call George upon arrival, as I'd agreed to. I decided to call now and let George talk to the boy.

I reached into my pocket, pulled out my cell phone and was about to make the call when Peter said, "What's that?"

"It's a cell phone. I'm going to call a friend of mine and I'll let you talk to him."

"What's a cell phone?"

It was then I looked around town again only to notice that there were no wires anywhere. "Peter, where did you live before you moved here?"

"Nowhere. I was born here."

"How old are you?"

"Seven. Well, I'm almost seven. I'll be seven in December."

I smiled. This was June 29. Close enough if you're a little kid ever anxious to get beyond childhood. Peter was so small I was suspicious of him telling me the truth. But then he was missing his front teeth. Maybe so, just small for his age!

"There's no electricity here, is there?"

"No, but I've heard of it," he smiled, obviously proud of himself.

So Peter is a child of the twentieth century; yet for all practical purposes, he might as well be born and raised in the Dark Ages. No radios, televisions, nor any of the other modern conveniences. No toys we've all come to take for granted! And now he was faced with a cell phone. How could I explain it to him? I realized I couldn't because I wasn't really sure how it worked myself. "Peter, I'm going to hit a bunch of numbers and if it works, we'll hear someone talking inside here. It's a kind of magic. Okay?"

"Okay," he said with a disbelieving wonderment in his eyes.

I punched in the proper numbers and it rang a couple of times before George picked up. I could barely hear him. He sounded like he was a million miles away. "Hello," he said.

His voice was weak. "George, this is Jake. I'm in the middle of Slippery Gulch."

"I can hardly hear you. Did you have any problems?"

"No, but that part along the cliff was exciting. There was no room for error." I chuckled a little and said, "I hope it's there when I go back." I was expecting a chuckle in return and an agreement on that, but what I got was hesitation and no chuckle. This kind of unnerved me.

"If you have any problems, give me a call. And call again when you're finished loading. The signal is really weak. I'm not sure how much longer these things are going to work."

"Yeah, I know," I said. "If I can't get through to you later, I'll see you in town this afternoon."

"Okay," he said and then added with genuine concern, "Be careful."

"Always, but before we hang up, there's someone here I want you to talk to."

"What did you say? Is someone else there with you?"

"Yeah, look, I found the footprints."

"You're kidding. Are they barefoot and little?"

"Yeah. Not only that, I have the source of those prints standing right next to me. His name is Peter Stevenson. He's six years old. He lives here, and his dad works in the mine. I'm going to have him say hello. Just a minute."

All this time Peter was looking at me as if I was nuts for standing there talking to myself. But not once did he interrupt. Either someone taught him some manners or he felt sorry for me because I was losing my mind. "Peter, I'm going to put this part of the phone up against your ear. When I do, say 'hello' nice and loud and then listen very carefully. Okay?"

"Will it hurt?" Peter asked.

I smiled and said, "Not at all." Curiosity apparently overcame his fear for he walked right up to me and allowed me to hold the phone against his ear. "Say 'hello' real loud."

He looked at me as if I was kidding him then said in a loud voice, "Hello."

George apparently heard him and said something back because Peter jumped a mile, looked at me in absolute amazement, and said, "There really is someone in there. How can he fit?"

I had to laugh. "The man isn't in there, just his voice. Say 'I'm Peter' and see what he says, but talk nice and loud."

So he said in a loud and amazed voice, "I'm Peter."

Peter said "Yeah....Yeah....I was born here....Yeah. Okay." At that, he handed the phone back to me and backed up a couple steps.

George said, "Jake, this doesn't make any—" and at that point the phone went dead. I said hello a couple of times but it was no use. I'd try again before leaving town but I doubted I'd get through until I got back to Basin Creek Road. Now I was really on my own. At any rate, it was time to get up to the mine. I looked down at Peter and said, "Peter, I have to walk up to the mine and take a look at the road. You want to walk with me?"

"No, I have to go." And with that he ran off. What a nice little kid. I smiled under a noonday sun that was really heating up my already cooked brain. My questions were at a boil.

# SEVEN

I started walking toward the intersection ahead of me when I heard someone call out, "Hey, honey, would you like to have some fun?"

I looked again toward the saloon and there, standing on the balcony above the swinging front doors, was a painted lady obviously ready for business. If I were in a truck stop, she'd be called a "lot lizard." She appeared to be in her early to mid-40s with long brown hair that looked dirty. She was way overweight. Her dress was ankle length, but she pulled her hem up to her knees, exposing her dust-laden plump legs, and said, "I come cheap!"

I thought to myself, "Yeah, I'll bet." I took one last look and headed back to the junction.

From the junction I started walking up the hill. I wanted to scope out the mine on the infamous Blood Run Road. As I continued, the hill got steeper and curved back and forth. Obviously Mike was wrong about there being just one curve. As I climbed, the drop off on my left became steeper. I didn't like the looks of this at all. I sure was hoping there'd be enough room at the top to turn my rig around because I certainly didn't want to back up this hill if I didn't have to, and I wasn't about to back down.

From the top, I got my second view of the mine, my first one close-up. Not much to look at, actually. There was a hole in the side of the hill reinforced with large timbers. It looked about the same as mines I remember seeing in cowboy movies in the 1950s. To the right of the mine were two small, wooden buildings that were actually not much more than cabins. Outside the farthest one to the right a horse was "parked." A horse? Yeah, that's what I said.

I stood there looking for any signs of a working mine such as a bulldozer or a front-end loader, but saw nothing. However, if Peter was right and the mine was closing down, I suppose the heavy equipment would already have been moved out. But there were no pickup trucks or cars in sight, just the horse.

It was time to make my presence known. I walked toward the building near the horse. As I passed it heading for a small, rickety porch, I patted its rump a couple of times. The dust flew. It ignored me. It didn't even move its ears to acknowledge my presence. I suspected it may have been an old nag but since I wasn't that familiar with horses, I really wasn't sure. I eyed the stairs suspiciously, wondering if they would support my weight. As I gingerly stepped on the first steps, one by one each pro-tested under my 138 pounds but held. The porch, no more than 4 feet across, groaned under both steps as well.

There were no signs outside the building to indicate that this was shipping and receiving or that it was even an office of any type. I knocked and waited for an answer. There was none, so I knocked again. Still no answer. I tried the doorknob. It turned but was in serious need of oil. I hesitantly opened the door and said hello. No answer! I opened the door wider and took one tentative step into the building. The small room was about 15 by 15 feet. There was only one crusty window and no artificial lighting of any type so the room was much darker than the outside. My eyes became adjusted as I looked around the room.

To my left was a small table with a wooden, three-drawer filing cabinet sitting on it. Next to the table was a wooden chair. Above the filing cabinet on the wall was a framed picture of something, but I couldn't make it out because of the dust coat-ing it. To my right was another wooden chair. Hanging from the ceiling was an old, unlit kerosene lantern again coated in a sheet of dust. Directly in front of me was a large, colonial rolltop desk with a man sitting in a swivel chair with his back to me.

The man spun his chair to face me—a middle-aged man with touches of gray in his hair, his full grizzly beard matching his bushy eyebrows, both shot through with white strands. He had a hard, deeply lined face with high cheekbones. His shoulders and chest spoke of power. His skin was pale and his eyes pierced mine without blinking. My first reaction was that if he had not moved I could swear he was dead.

I asked, "Are you Jeremiah Peabody?"

"Yeah. What the hell do you want?"

So much for mountain hospitality. I always go into a place with a good, positive attitude and try to maintain it throughout, but I could see this guy was going to make it difficult.

"I'm Jake Winters from QZX. I'm here to pick up a load going to Smith and Associates in Reno, Nevada."

"Oh, okay. You have a big wagon? This is a heavy load."

"How heavy is heavy?"

"Four thousands pounds heavy."

Did I detect a trace of humor in this man? His eyes registered no life much less good humor. Since a 4,000-pound load isn't even enough to feel behind the wheel, I struggled to keep a straight face. "I think I can handle it. Where do you want my wagon?"

"Where is it now?"

"It's down in the town below."

"Well, what's the damn thing doing down there? You expect me to carry that thing down to you? Get it up here! I want to see it."

"Where do you want it?"

"Just get it up here and I'll tell you then."

"Can't! I have to know now where so I can maneuver it once I get it up here."

He looked at me as if I was the dumbest, most incompetent slob he'd ever met. "Okay," he said. "Did you see the wooden tripod to the right of the mine shaft when you walked in?"

"I think so. It's a tripod with a pole coming out of the top of it and an arm coming out of the top of the pole?"

"Yeah, that's it."

"What is that thing?"

I could see this question only confirmed my questionable intelligence. "It's a loader. What the hell did you think it was? You ever haul from a mine before?"

I didn't want to give my inexperience away so I changed the subject quick. "Why don't you just use a forklift?"

"What the hell is a forklift? You mean a pitchfork for pitching horseshit out of a stall? We got no stalls around here and only one horse."

He's got to be kidding me, I thought, yet dared not say it. But looking at his eyes, I could tell he wasn't. "A forklift is a machine with a couple of flat bars in front. You slip the bars under the object you want to lift and load it into the back of the wagon. It makes life easier." There was no response. "Makes the work go faster." Still no sign of life. "Saves time, don't you see?"

"Forget it. This is a small operation. We got no fancy stuff like that. We got a small crusher period. Can't afford a larger one! We don't need a larger one! We don't need a pitchfork lifter let alone a pitchfork."

"What's a crusher?"

I could tell I'd just slid a step closer to total stupidity. "We put the raw material out of the ground into a crusher and grind it into a powdery substance. Then we ship it to a smelter to be formed into ingots for shipping. Since I'm closing down the mine, I'm selling the crusher to my brother. His business is in Reno. He's got a buyer for it. Now are you happy?"

I had to get frank with the man. "I didn't mean to pry. I have no experience whatsoever in mining. Just curious what a crusher was. Thanks for explaining that."

"Thanks for being up front. I about wrote you off as plum stupid." I ignored the compliment.

"Okay, I'll back my wagon up to the tripod and we'll get her loaded." I wasn't sure why he continued to refer to my truck as a wagon, but I humored him. It wasn't all that unusual. A flatbed with removable sides and a tarp over the top is referred to as a covered wagon. When we pull into a DOT scale we say they're just "weighing our wagon." We refer to an ambulance as a meat wagon. So there are many terms in the trucking industry that comes out of the past two centuries. A bus is a stagecoach. The term teamster comes from the horse and buggy days. In the 1800s, a teamster controlled and steered the team of horses that pulled his wagon, thus a teamster. I figured the language of mining was about as mixed-up between the past and present as in the trucking industry.

"I'll go down and get the wagon and be back up in a few minutes." I walked outside, patted the unmoving horse again as I went by, and took one more look around. As I walked to the little town, I pondered on a plan. If I backed up the road, then once I got to the top, it would be easy to back up to the tripod. However, backing up that hill would not be the smartest thing I'd ever done. There were two different places I'd have to back, blind side around a curve with a cliff on my blind side. With no one to help, that plan was a recipe for disaster. Driving the truck up forward would be safer but would make for a lot of hard work at the top. In maneuvering the truck into the right position, at least I'd get there. I opted for plan two.

## EIGHT

Scoping out the curves on the walk back to my truck I was convinced I'd made the right decision. The sun was overhead. I was sweating enough that I looked forward to firing up the air conditioner in my cab. I climbed into the truck, started it, and locked in the differential. This gave me eight-wheel drive instead of four, for better traction. In third gear I headed for the intersection, put on my left signal, and made the turn. I had to laugh at myself for signaling in a ghost town. (I got into that habit when first driving a car at age sixteen, a habit far too few Americans have these days.)

I made the turn to start up the hill, keeping it at about 4 or 5 miles per hour. Too fast and I'd go into a power skid and over the edge; too slow and I'd come to a complete stop. In the loose dirt, I might not get it started. I sure didn't want to have to back up and start over again.

As I approached the first curve I was thrilled I'd already slid my tandems all the way forward. The first curve was the worst. The trailer tires went up on the right side of the hill a little and forced the trailer to lean toward the edge. The steer tires were dangerously close to the edge but I made it. The rest of the curves were less sharp, but the incline of the hill increased to about 12 percent. A couple of times I lost traction and almost came to a complete stop. Both times the truck thankfully dug in and let me creep along. At last the top! After maneuvering and loading, all that was left was getting back down in one piece.

The trick maneuvering the truck around to get the trailer to where it had to be wasn't easy. It was 75 feet long and required a lot of forward and backward motion. A driver can get so frustrated, he'd just like to get out, walk to the back of the trailer, pick it up, and move it to where he'd like it. Short of that, all you can do is keep seesawing until it's where it has to be to load.

As I opened up the trailer doors, Peabody came along with his horse. "It's about time you got that rig up here," he said. "I don't have all day, you know."

My attitude was quickly going south with this guy. What was his hurry? At this point I really wanted to tell Peabody what he could kiss, but I just kept my mouth shut. I would get loaded quickly and get out of here.

"Wait until I lift up the crusher. Then you back your wagon right between the front legs of the tripod."

The logs that made up this machine were huge. He took his horse to the opposite side of this contraption and tied a rope to a special harness he had attached to the horse. The rope went to a large steel ring somehow planted in the ground, then up to the beam. The end of the beam closest to the horse was far up in the air, the opposite end resting on the crusher so the beam was at a 45 degree angle to the ground. Although the horse was huge, I just couldn't imagine any horse being able to lift 2 tons of crusher. Then I looked at the top of this crazy thing and for the first time noticed a series of pulleys that the rope went through and thought, well maybe. I stood there in amazement.

The horse, without appearing to strain in the least, walked away from the tripod. As it did, the end of the beam closest to the horse lowered while the far end raised taking the crusher with it. The crusher was just high enough to slip it into my trailer. "Okay, start backing," Peabody said.

"Just watch the back of the wagon. I don't want to back over the tripod. When I get close, stop me."

"Don't worry, I know what I'm doing."

"You could have fooled me," I said as I was walking back to my tractor. I climbed in, released the air brakes, and looked in the mirrors to see where Peabody was. He was nowhere in sight. I sat there and waited for a minute, but he didn't appear. I set the brakes, climbed back out, and wandered back to see what he was doing. He was standing directly behind the trailer with his horse. As I rounded the back of the trailer he looked at me and said, "What the hell are you doing?"

"I couldn't see you in my mirrors so I came back to see what you were doing."

"I was going to direct you backwards, if you ever decided to back up."

"Well, stand off to the side. I have to be able to see you. I never back up when someone is standing directly behind me. It's a safety thing!"

Once again I climbed back into my tractor, muttering to myself. I looked in the left mirror and sure enough, there was Peabody. I looked toward the right mirror out of habit, but was distracted by a small form. It was Peter, laughing. I figured he was laughing at the problems I was having with Peabody. I started my truck, released the brakes, shifted into reverse, and looked back to where Peter had been, but he was gone. I thought briefly of Mike's small footprints but then I looked in the left mirror again and there was Peabody; the images of the small prints were gone.

I slowly started backing, watching for hand motions from Peabody, but saw none. His mouth was moving. He couldn't possibly believe I could hear him over the noise of the truck, could he? The tripod was so large I could back the trailer right under it to the crusher itself. But I had to know when to stop so I wouldn't hit it. Just then Peabody motioned with both hands to stop. I set the brakes, got down, and walked back.

"I was yelling for you to stop, but you just kept backing up," Peabody said. "What's wrong with you?"

"No problem, it's perfect." The two sides of the trailer were within inches of the two front legs of the tripod, and the arm extending from the top of the tripod was positioned perfectly inside the trailer. I couldn't have done it better with proper help if I'd had it.

"You almost ran over it."

"Almost doesn't count. Let's get this thing loaded."

He directed the horse to back slowly. The crusher slowly lowered to the floor 5 feet from the back doors. I could hardly believe it: The darn thing worked. He didn't need a forklift after all. He unhooked the horse, and I unhooked the rope attached to the rope under the crusher. That rope would have to stay.

"Do you have some 2-by-4s, nails, and a hammer?"

"What for?" he said.

"To secure the load. I want to make sure this thing doesn't slide forwards, backwards, or to the side going up and down the hills."

I could tell he knew I was right. I could also tell he hated to admit it so he didn't. He walked away and in a few minutes came back with my request.

Each 2-by-4 was about 4 feet long. I threw the wood into the trailer, placed the nails, really small spikes, and hammer in the back, crawled in and proceeded to secure the wood. Six spikes in each 2-by-4 surrounding the crusher meant that the contraption wasn't going anywhere. I would have preferred it farther back in the trailer, but weighing only 4,000 pounds meant I wouldn't feel it no matter where it was in the trailer.

"After you finish up playing around out here, come in the office and sign the paperwork, then you can get the hell out of my mine."

"No problem. Be there in a minute!" I groaned. I finished securing the last of the 2-by-4s, moved around to the front of the truck, crawled into the tractor, started it, and pulled out 7 or 8 feet, then went back and closed the trailer doors.

I had just completed latching the last door when I heard a small voice say, "Hey, Jake. See, what did I tell you? He's a mean one, ain't he?"

"Yeah, you were right, Peter, he sure is," I said to Peter Stevenson. "What are you doing here?"

"My daddy said he's going to get even with old man Peabody today or tomorrow."

"How's he going to do it?"

"I don't know. All I know is it has something to do with a wagon and a crusher in it. You got a crusher in there don't ya?"

"Yes, I do. But if your daddy's going to do something, he'd better do it quick. I'm leaving in a few minutes. You think he's going to do something here?"

"I don't know when or where. I just heard him say he was going to do something."

"Did your daddy tell you this?"

"Nah, he don't tell me nothing. All he does is beat me. I was hiding in town just now and I heard him tell some other guy. I was real scared. If he found out I knew and was telling someone, he'd kill me." He began trembling again. "I hate my dad."

"Peter, come here for a minute."

He looked at me with a terrified expression. "You ain't going to hit me, are you?"

I smiled at him assuredly. "No, Peter, I don't hit kids."

He walked over to me slowly. I knelt down to his level and gently put my hand on his shoulder. I could tell he was ready to bolt at the slightest sign of aggression. He felt cool to the touch. I said, "Peter, how long has it been since you had a good meal?"

Looking down at the ground he said, "I don't remember."

I put my hand under his chin and lifted his head slightly so I could look into his eyes. What I saw unnerved me. This was the most scared and saddest little boy I had ever seen. "Peter, I've got some cookies up front. Will you stay here until I get back? I'll only be a minute."

His eyes brightened slightly above a faint hint of a smile. "Okay," he said.

"Promise?" I said. "I'll only be a minute."

"I promise."

I went up to my tractor and grabbed a package of chocolate chip cookies and my water bottle and walked to the back of the trailer. Peter was there waiting. I opened the cookies. He tore into them as if they were the first form of food he'd seen in weeks. For all I knew, they were.

I stood there and watched him eat for a minute. Then I handed him the water bottle and he tried to drink it so fast it ran down his chin to his filthy chest and stomach. I took the bottle from him and told him to slow down or he'd get sick. I gave it back and he slowed down some. At that point I said, "You overheard your daddy talking to another man about doing something to a load coming out of J and J Mines, right?"

He simply muttered, "Ugh huh," as he continued to devour my cookies.

"Do you know who the other man was?"

"No, I never seen him before, but he was right big and he looked even meaner than old man Peabody."

"Did you hear them say they were going to do something on the road?"

"I'm not sure."

"Did you hear them say what they were going to do?"

"No, I got real scared and ran away. If daddy saw me there, he'd kill me."

"Well look, I thank you for telling me about this. I'll keep my eyes open and be real careful. I am going to have to talk to Peabody about this and let him know of the possible threats."

"No, you can't," he said hysterically, tears forming in his eyes. "If my daddy finds out I told, he'll kill me."

Peter looked absolutely pathetic. He was crying hard now with tears streaming down his grubby cheeks and taking particles of dirt with them. As he tried to wipe some of the tears away, the dirt was spread around his face to make him look even worse. I took a handkerchief from my back pocket, dampened it and wiped off his face and neck. He was looking better but still crying and scared, so I picked him up and held him for a few minutes.

"Peter, I have to talk to Peabody and the law enforcement officials and let them know of the possible dangers. This load is going from one state to another. That makes it federal. I, being the driver, am responsible for this load from here to Reno, Nevada. If I learn of possible problems pertaining to the transport of this load, it is my responsibility to report that to the shipper, to the law, and to my company. If I didn't report this and something happens to this load, I will be in very big trouble. I don't know how much of what I just said you understand, but Peter, I don't have a choice."

"But if my daddy finds out, he'll kill me."

"I don't think he'll kill you, Peter."

"You don't understand. He hates me. My mommy died when I was being born and he has always blamed me ever since. He says if I wasn't born, mommy wouldn't be dead now."

I know young children tend to exaggerate. It was obvious Peter was a neglected child but I seriously doubted if Mr. Stevenson would kill his own son. Nevertheless, I had to try and get Peter some help. In the meantime, I was running out of time.

Just then Jeremiah yelled from the small office, "Hey, driver, are you going to come in and sign these damn bills or not?"

"Yeah, I'll be right there."

Peter tightened his grip around my neck at the sound of Peabody's voice. I moved the hair from his face. "Peter, I have to get going, but I'm going to talk to some friends of mine in Basin and get you some help. Thanks for the warning and I'll watch my step. And you watch yours too, okay?" He nodded his head but said nothing.

I set him down and ruffled his long filthy hair. He turned to leave but then turned back and stuck out his small hand and we shook. I had to admit, I was impressed. Where did a little backwoods kid learn that? "Be careful, Peter, and thanks again."

"You be careful, too, Jake," and with that he was gone. I stood there wishing there were something more I could do for him. Absolutely nothing came to mind at the moment.

## NINE

I walked up to the front of my truck, grabbed a seal, seal manifest, and lock, and walked into the office. Peabody was sitting in his chair waiting for me. He did not appear to be in a good mood. In other words, it did not appear that his mood had changed at all since I'd first seen him.

"What the hell took you so long?" he asked. I wondered what he was like when he was mad. I decided I didn't want to find out. "I was talking to a little boy. I thought you—"

"I don't pay you to talk to brats."

Now he was starting to get my dander up. "Peabody," I said angrily, "you should have stopped before the last two words, then you would have been right."

He looked at me disoriented and barked out, "What?"

I repeated myself and added "You don't pay me, my company does. I'll talk to anyone I want to, but that little boy told me something that should interest you."

He suddenly looked at me with a small amount of interest. "Who was he?"

"Peter Stevenson. He said his dad works here."

"Peter Stevenson? You were talking to that stinking kid? You can't believe a word he says. His dad don't work for me no more. All he ever done was drink and slap his kid around. Now I don't care much about that snot-nosed brat. Lord knows, if he was mine, I'd beat him myself. When you work for me, you come in sober and leave sober."

"So you fired the boy's father?"

"You're damn right I fired him. Wouldn't you?"

49

"Yeah, I suppose I would. However, the 'brat' has information you need to know." I then related what Peter had told me.

"Look, that kid's a little liar," Peabody countered. "Even if what he said is true, his father is so drunk all the time, he'd never be able to come up with no plan, let alone carry it out."

"Any chance of getting help for the boy?"

"What for?"

I looked at him. Was he blind or did he just not care? "He's being physically abused and neglected. The poor kid is starving to death."

"Good. Then we'll be rid of him."

I looked at this cold, angry man hardly believing what I'd just heard. "How can you say that? He's just a little kid."

"He's a little pain in the ass. Look, what a man does to his wife and kids is nobody's business but his own. Now are you going to sign this bill and get out of here?"

I could see there was no sense in continuing a conversation along these lines with an individual living in the Dark Ages. I took the bill and looked it over. I'd never seen a bill like this before. The entire bill was handwritten. Everything except the weight seemed to be there, so I thought it was legal, just unusual. Before signing I asked Peabody to include the weight.

"Why, I told you how much it weighs."

"Yes, but the DOT doesn't know. If I get stopped, they like to see the weight of the load on the bills."

"What's the DOT?"

This guy was really out of it. "The Department of Transportation." I turned the bill around so it was facing him. "Just write 'weight' right here and then write '4,000 pounds.'"

"Okay," he said and did as I requested. I signed both his and my copies of the bill as I said, "Peabody, I'm going to put a seal on the wagon, and I have to have you sign what's called a seal manifest. By signing that form, all you're saying is you witnessed me putting a seal on the wagon."

"What seal?"

I pulled out a long, narrow aluminum strip from my left shirt pocket and said, "This is a seal. I'll slip this through a couple of loops in the door handle and lock it. Why don't we come out to the wagon where I can better show you how it works."

Reluctantly he agreed. He wasn't really interested in leaving the office, but he was curious. We walked to the back of the trailer where I showed him a small latch that comes down over the handle. The hole in the latch fits over the hole in the handle. I slipped the seal through both holes then slipped one end of the seal into the other end until I heard a slight click. I gave it a good yank to secure it. It was secure. I put the lock on and was set to roll. All I needed was Peabody's John Hancock on my seal manifest. Taking out the form, I handed it to him and explained again that his signature simply indicated he witnessed me putting the seal on the trailer. He took the form and said he'd have to run back inside to sign it, his pen and ink were on his desk. I took out my pen and handed it to him.

He just stood there looking at it. Finally he took it and asked, "Will this write?"

"Try it. It's a pen. It's a reliable ballpoint." I reached over and pushed on the end and said, "There you go. Sign right here." I was trying to remember my American history and the settlement of the Wild West. Ballpoint pens had been around for at least 50 years now.

Peabody looked at it and said, "Where's the ink?"

"Inside. Take the pen and move the small point over the form. It'll write." I looked at him. "Where have you been? Ballpoint pens are as old as me. Just sign this form right here and I'll be on my way."

He signed and stood staring at the business end of the pen with eyebrows raised in wonderment. "This is really something. You wouldn't happen to have another one of these, would you?"

For the first time the man addressed me in a civil manner. "That's my good Parker but I have a cheap one. Here. It's yours." I exchanged pens with him but his eyes followed my Parker into my shirt pocket. "Nice meeting you, Peabody." I didn't think he caught my sarcasm.

"Wait a minute, driver."

I really wanted to leave, to get as far away from Peabody as soon as possible. "What do you want now?"

"I was wondering if you could do a favor for me once you get to Reno."

I couldn't believe what I was saying in reply. "Okay, I'll try. What do you have in mind?"

"If you would, deliver this letter to my brother, Jacob. I haven't seen him in several years. You'll see him. He's the president of Smith and Associates."

Oh Lord, I thought, not another Peabody. "Is he anything like you?" I asked.

"No, he don't know the first thing about bossin' a job. He's soft."

"Okay," I said. "Give me the letter. I'll deliver it for you."

He pulled a piece of paper from a pocket, handed it to me and said, "Thanks," turned, and walked into his office. That's the last time I ever saw Jeremiah Peabody. I walked back to my tractor, climbed into the cab and placed the bill of lading, the seal manifest, and Peabody's letter into a trip envelope. The envelope is for any and all paperwork pertaining to a trip. This way a driver keeps organized. Plus I only get paid by sending it into the company along with my log sheets from the trip and any receipts.

I started the engine and just sat there thinking about this mind-boggling experience. I came to a ghost town that now has a few people living in it, loaded at a ghost mine that is now being worked again on a limited basis before closing down soon. And it's being managed by one of the strangest individuals I've ever met. And I had run into a little boy in serious trouble, who desperately needed help. I only hoped I could get him that help soon. All I had to do was get out of here in one piece before I could get him help. I owed him one for his heads up to me about possible dangers ahead.

# TEN

I released the air brakes, and started a forward and backward motion just to get to the point where I could make the turn out of the mine area and onto the hill leading back down to town. I put it in first, or creeper gear, and crept along at about 1 mile an hour. The most minuscule slide could have disastrous consequences. It took about 15 minutes to go that quarter mile back to town. At least I made it.

I made a wide right turn from Blood Run Road onto Main Street, or whatever it was called, and crawled alone in third gear at about 3 miles per hour.

The street was void of all life. Perhaps the old man got to wherever he was going. Perhaps the painted lady was busy, and perhaps Peter was hiding someplace. A cross-country driver has different individuals always stepping into and out of his life for brief periods of time, never to be seen again. At any rate, I was finally on my way.

As I was creeping through town, thinking about all of this, I thought I caught a slight movement in front and to my right, but when I looked, there was nothing. Maybe I was just imagining things. Still I wondered. When I got up to the spot, I stopped, turned off the truck, and got out. I walked to where I thought I caught the movement but no one was there. I looked down at the ground and there were small bare footprints in the dirt. Peter? I looked beyond to see where they'd come from but they hadn't. They started right there. I followed them into an alley to see where he was going but after I went about 40 feet, they just stopped. How on earth could Peter or whoever leave such tracks? There were no nearby doors or windows to walk or crawl into nor anything to swing into. A chill ran down my spine. Mike's phantom footprints? Only a prankster or ghost could leave such tracks and it was obvious Peter was not a ghost. The chill returned. I stood there and yelled, "Peter, come out here. I want to say goodbye to you." A wee voice yelled back, "I fooled you, Jake."

"You sure did, Peter. Now come on out."

Suddenly I felt a slight tug on my back pocket. I turned around and there he was, all filthy but with a clean face. I pointed down at the tracks and said, "Peter, are these your tracks?"

Looking as though he may be in trouble, he sheepishly said, "Yeah."

"How do you do this?"

"Do what?"

"Peter, your tracks come back into this alley and just stop right here. Where did you go?"

There was confusion on his face. "I don't know, I just kept going, I think. Yeah, I did. See, there are my tracks."

I turned back and sure enough, there were his tracks continuing to the end of the alley and then turning right, around the building. But I was sure they had ended right here. Or was I thinking of Mike's footprints and let my imagination get the better of me? Then I thought of how they just started the same way they ended. I turned around and followed the tracks back to the street. But they hadn't just started there. They started across the street somewhere. In one respect I thought I was going crazy, but I realized it had to be my imagination.

I turned around and looked down at Peter, then knelt down so I was at his level and said "Peter, I have to get going, but I have really enjoyed talking to you. Can you tell me any more about any dangers ahead for either you or me?"

"No! Do you have to?"

"Yeah, I do. Peter, before I go, I'd like to take your picture. Is that okay with you?" I wondered why I hadn't taken any at the mine. Although Peabody was an idiot, he was nevertheless a colorful character. And the loading of the crusher with the horse and that contraption Peabody used would have made a great picture. Nobody would believe me without such a photo.

"What's a picture?" Peter asked, bringing me out of my thoughts.

I thought about that for a moment: Being only six and being born in this small, backwoods mining community, it was possible he'd never seen a camera before. I explained, "A picture is a small impression of you on a piece of paper. You can look at it and see yourself. That way I can always look at that little piece of paper and see you."

"Does it hurt?"

He was always concerned about pain, perhaps for a good reason. "No, it doesn't hurt at all," I assured him, smiling.

"Well, okay."

"Good, stay right there. I'll be right back." I climbed into my truck and grabbed my camera. When I climbed back out, Peter was still there looking a little concerned as he observed my camera. "Don't worry, Peter, I'm not going to hurt you and this camera won't either," I said reassuringly.

The first picture I took recorded a lot of fear and sadness in his eyes, which was certainly accurate. After the click, I said, "Now that wasn't so bad, was it?"

"You did it already?"

"Yeah, I did it." When you hear the click, that's it. Now I want to take at least one more of you." I pulled the camera up and said, "Now give me a big smile." He didn't. He continued to stand there with the same mixture of fear and sadness. "Peter, if you don't give me a big smile, I'm going to tickle you." That got a hint of a smile. From what he'd told me he hadn't had many reasons to smile in his short life. I put the camera down, walked over to him, turned him sideways to me and started tickling him in the ribs. At first all I got was a giggle, but soon he was laughing hysterically. I doubted he'd ever laughed like that before. It was good for him. I quickly picked up the camera and got a picture of a smile that was already starting to fade. So I said, "Remember your ribs!" Instantly I got the shot I wanted: a huge smile with his two front teeth missing. "Well, Peter, I've got to get going."

"Do you have to?"

"I really do."

"Could you take me with you?"

"No, I can't. I can't take any passengers under the age of 12."

"I sure wish I could go with you. When will you be back?"

I knew my chances of getting back were slim to none, but I couldn't tell him that. So I just told him I'd be back as soon as I could.

Shyly he asked, " Could you tickle me one more time?"

I laughed. "Sure, why not?" So I crouched down, put him on my knee, and gave him a good tickling. He laughed even harder than before. Then I stood up and said, "I must get going. I don't have a choice." Looking down at him, I saw the tears starting. I realized a goodbye handshake wouldn't make it. I picked him up, gave him a hug, and said, "Peter, be a good boy and watch your step, okay? And in the meantime, I'm going to try my best to get you some help and maybe get you out of here." I wiped away the tears, put him down, ruffled his hair, and headed for the truck. Suddenly, I felt as if I'd known this kid for 100 years.

Before I got to the truck I turned around and said, "Peter, when I get to the top of that hill," I pointed to the hill outside of town, "I'm going to stop and take a picture of the town. I'll wave to you one last time from there, okay?" He nodded his head but said nothing. I climbed in, started up, released the brakes, hooked my seat belt, and headed for Basin. As I slowly drove past Peter, I looked down at him, said goodbye again, and waved. He still didn't say anything but waved a little. The tears were now running down his cheeks and neck but also starting to work their way down his grimy chest. It was a truly sorry sight—a tragic comedy rolled up into one lonely, little boy.

# ELEVEN

When almost to the top of the hill, I stopped the Babes, set the brakes, grabbed the camera, and got out. Looking back into town, I saw what looked like one very small, lonely, and sad figure standing in the middle of the street. I put the zoom lens on and took a quick picture. I waved and got a small, quick wave back. But then Peter turned and darted into the alley and was gone, probably forever. After all, when would I have an opportunity to get back to Slippery Gulch? I was sure Peter would become one more individual that stepped quickly into my life for a short period of time and then quickly exited, never to be seen again. With a little luck, though, my friends would be able to get in here in time, rescue him, and get him out.

As I walked back to the Babes something hit. A feeling! I didn't understand it but I suddenly felt genuinely concerned. I stood overlooking Peter's town and prayed for his safety. I also prayed that someday he would find the friend and happiness he so richly deserved.

Once in the cab, I punched into my computer all the information pertaining to the load, and settled down to drive. I was looking forward to the trip because it was a beautiful run all the way. I'd take I-15 to Salt Lake City where I'd pick up I-80 right into Reno. However, before I got to that enjoyable part of the trip, I still had a little cliff to contend with. I took one last look back at the town in my mirrors and headed for the cliff.

Once there, I got out and took a picture of the cliff with the right side of my truck in the foreground, then walked across to the other side and took a shot looking back toward the truck.

The road was narrower than I recalled. I walked to the edge to remind myself how straight down it was for 100 feet. I did it once before, I guessed I could do it again. I walked back, climbed in, said a little prayer, and started inching forward through the "dead zone." The warning Peter had given me did cross my mind. Two hundred yards of raw nerves! One little mistake and it would all be over, and quickly!

Creeping along with my left tires right on the edge, watching a few rocks disappear over the edge, I had an urge to floor it. I resisted. I was wet in sweat. Keeping a snail's pace, I hung onto the steering wheel as if it were a safety rope. Unlike my first pass I was sitting 8 feet above ground level, literally on the edge where I could see all the way to the bottom.

My front tires reached firm ground first, then The Babes, and in my mirror I saw the last tires make it home free. My underwear? Still clean.

The rest of the way back to Basin Creek Road would be a piece of cake. I never want another pickup like this one. If I ever return to Slippery Gulch, it will be in *my* pickup.

I stopped at the overgrown intersection and called George. A man answered and I said, "George?"

"No, this is Mike."

"Oh, that's okay. This is Jake."

"Jake, what's going on? What happened? Where are you? What took you so long?"

"Whoa! Wait a minute. Slow down. It was a slow drive in and out and slow up to the mine. But I got the load. And I met the source of your footprints."

"Yeah, that's what George said. How far away are you?"

"About 20 minutes."

"George will be back in 10 and Jane should be here any minute. Watch your step."

"Always," I said and hung up. I put on my left signal and pulled wide through the intersection, keeping her on the road. When I got down to Main Street and the Basin Post Office, I turned right and drove past the saloon, blowing my air horn. I went down to the end of town, did a turnaround, and parked in front of the saloon. All three were outside waiting for me.

I turned her off, set everything, and went around to where they were all waiting. Jane said, "We were all real worried Jake. I was just getting ready to send Mike up there to see if you were okay."

"What's the problem? It's just 5:00 your time."

"I wasn't worried," George said with chuckle, "but was that you or who on the phone? I could barely hear."

"That was Peter Stevenson. He was the reason I took so long. He was born in Slippery Gulch almost 6 years ago. His father worked in the mine but was just recently fired for drinking. He beat the boy a lot, from what Peter said. This kid needs help. He's barely clothed and rather malnourished."

"Wait a minute," Mike said. "This just doesn't make any sense at all. I've been up there many times in the last 6 years. Nobody's been living there and no one has been working the mine."

"Mike, I don't know what to tell you, but Peter wasn't the only person I saw. An old man yelled at me for leaving my truck in the middle of the road. I was propositioned by a lady of the night, and I heard piano music and laughter coming from the saloon. And of course there was Jeremiah Peabody."

"What about Peabody? What was he like?" Mike asked.

"Wait a minute," Jane said. "Before you answer, you must be starving. It's 8:00 your time. How about some dinner?"

"No, that isn't necessary but thanks anyway," I said.

"I know it isn't," she said. "Now how about a New York strip, a baked potato, and some corn? How do you want it done?"

She wasn't going to take no for an answer. Besides, I was starving. I hadn't eaten a thing all day since Peter ate my cookies. "Medium will be fine. Thanks, Jane. I guess I am a little hungry. Sorry, Mike, what was your question?"

"What was Peabody like?"

"Weird and nasty!"

"How so?" George asked.

"Well, as a good example: I had him come out to the truck with me to sign my seal manifest. When he borrowed my pen, he was amazed. He'd never seen a ballpoint before. Had no idea how it worked either."

"You're kidding," Mike said.

"No, I'm serious. And he had no idea what the DOT was. And when he looked into the back of my trailer, he said, 'My God, that's the biggest Pittsburgh I'd ever seen.' Whatever a Pittsburgh is."

They all looked at each other and Mike volunteered, "You've never heard of a Pittsburgh?"

"The city, sure but never 'a' Pittsburgh."

"A Pittsburgh was a large freight wagon, used in these parts until about World War I when it was slowly replaced by trucks. In these mountains, it was generally pulled by 10 to 20 horses or mules."

"Well, maybe he had a sense of humor after all," I said.

"Maybe," Mike said thoughtfully.

"Here's another example of his meanness: When I asked him if he could get the boy some help, he said, 'What for?' When I explained to him that Peter was apparently starving to death, he said 'Good, maybe he won't last much longer.'"

"Good Lord, he actually said that?" Jane interrupted.

"Yeah, he's got to be one of the cruelest individuals I've ever had the pleasure of meeting." I then told them about Peter's fear that his father would kill him if he knew that Peter was warning me of a threat on my safety in getting out.

"Mike, we've got to go to Slippery Gulch tomorrow and get that kid out of there," Jane urged, starting to put my steak on.

"Jane, we can't just go in there and grab him," Mike said. "That would be kidnapping."

"Yeah, you're right. I'll call Beth Jackson later on. I'm sure once she hears what's going on, she'll want to go in with us."

"Who's Beth Jackson?" I asked.

"A good friend of mine and a social worker for the county," Jane said. "I think she will be very interested and concerned to learn what's going on up there. She should be able to get a deputy sheriff to go along."

"Okay, we'll take a drive up there tomorrow," Mike said. "Besides I'd like to meet Peabody and see why his name sounds so familiar."

"Yeah, I'd like to go myself, but I can't," George said. "I've got tax work to do tomorrow. I'll be interested in hearing what you have to say. By the way, Jake, what did you pick up?"

"A crusher."

"A crusher?" Mike asked. "And you fit that thing in your truck?"

"Yeah," I said kind of puzzled at his question. "It isn't that big. It's only 2 tons."

"You're kidding," Mike said. "Let me take a look at this thing."

"No can do, Mike. I've got a seal on the truck. Peabody signed the seal manifest and I registered the number in the computer. I can't take it off."

Jane brought my meal to me. "What would you like to drink?"

"Coffee is fine. I feel bad about eating in front of you."

"You should," George said with a wink. "The way she took over, you'd think she owned this place."

"I do own half of it, big brother, and don't you ever forget it," Jane said.

"How can I? You won't let me." George said.

If a person were blind, this little discussion between brother and sister would have sounded serious. However, seeing the twinkle in their eyes it was obvious it was good-natured jabbing.

"Well what does it look like?" George asked referring to the crusher.

"It's about 4 feet long, 3 feet high and 2 to 2½ feet wide and it has a wooden wheel, like an old wagon wheel on either side of it."

"That sounds like something right out of a museum. Didn't you say it was going to some place in Reno?" George asked.

"Yeah, that's right, a place called Smith and Associates. I don't know what kind of business it is, but I did find out that Peabody's brother, Jacob, owns the business."

61

"Oh you're kidding," Mike said. "So you can't even get away from the Peabodys in Reno?"

"Yeah, that's the way it looks. You know, something else that's strange about this whole thing is the bill of lading."

"Why?" asked Jane." What's strange about that?"

"Come on out to the truck. I'll show you."

After finishing my delicious meal, we walked out to my truck and I produced both the bill of lading and the seal manifest. In looking at the bill of lading they all could see the rarity of the document immediately. "The entire bill is written out in longhand," Jane said. "Aren't they always done by computer these days?"

"Yes, always," I said. "Slippery Gulch doesn't have electricity but there is such a thing as a typewriter."

"Yeah, this is weird," Jane said. She looked at the seal manifest and asked, "The number on the manifest corresponds with the number on the seal I assume?" I nodded. "What does the seal look like?"

Come around to the back of the trailer. We walked to the back where I pointed out the seal. "This is only one example of a seal. There are many types but their purpose is to discourage would-be thieves and let the driver see quickly if there has been any tampering. Other types are thick wire and a very heavy piece of steel. You can only get them off with a good set of cable cutters. You find them on expensive loads such as computers."

Jane looked at the number on the seal closely and compared it to the number on the manifest. I continued. "Once the truck is sealed and the witness has signed the manifest, I register the number with my company on my computer. If at any time during the trip I find the seal gone or if by chance the number is different, I know immediately the load has been tampered with."

Once again George and Mike looked at the witness' signature. George said, "Jeremiah Peabody. Where have I heard that name before? Jake, would you mind if I make a copy of this? In fact, while I'm at it, would you mind if I make a copy of the bill of lading too?"

"Well, I can't see why not, but why do you want copies?"

"Yeah, that's what I was wondering, George?" Mike said.

"I know why." Jane said. "He has always been like this ever since he was about 8 years old. He'd go around looking for little weird things and then try to turn it into a mystery."

"All he had to do was look in a mirror! But then there's no mystery about his weird puss!" Mike laughed at George's expense, but George wasn't laughing.

"Mike," he said, "How many times have you been up there in the last 6 years?"

"Oh, I don't know. Three, maybe four times."

"How about you, Jane?" George asked.

"I've only been up there once. I went up with Mike about 4 years ago."

"Did either of you see a lady of the night, a little kid, or an old miner?" George asked. "Or did either of you hear noises coming from the saloon? Did either of you see Peabody working the mine?"

I was about to say something, but Mike beat me to it. "No, but I saw those little footprints on my last trip."

"Or you thought you did," George said. "And they freaked you out so bad you haven't been back since."

Mike started to counter George's attack but I butted in. "Now, George, I can't say what Mike saw, but I know what I saw and heard. And in fact, you talked to that kid yourself on the phone."

Jane said with a harsh voice, "George, back off."

George looked at Jane then at Mike and finally at me. "Jake and Mike, I apologize. I didn't mean to accuse either one of you of fabricating anything, but something is going on here. Both Mike and I have been in there several times in the past 6 years and have never seen any sign of life, except for your last time in there, Mike, when you said you saw a child's tracks. Then out of the blue, Jake's company gets a call from Peabody. He wants a truck to come in and pick up a load of something. Jake goes in and sees all kinds of people, and I talk to a little kid on the phone."

"So what are you saying?" Jane asked.

"I think there's been some kind of a backwoods cult that's been living in there for a number of years, and now they've decided to move. They decide they need some money for the move, come up with an antique crusher and find a buyer. It's just a theory, but anybody have any better explanation?"

"If there's been a cult living there, then why haven't we ever seen anybody when we've been there," Mike said. "And how do you explain the footprints that start no place and then just stop?"

"If a person doesn't want to be seen, he won't be," George said. "As far as the tracks go, anybody can make their tracks disappear if they want to. If it is a cult that doesn't want visitors…and wants to spook nosy folks like you…well."

"Then why did I see so many people up there today?" I asked.

"I don't really know. Unless they figured they were leaving soon, and it doesn't matter anymore," George conjectured.

"But George," I said, "Peter, the little boy, told me they were closing the mine. He said that his dad had worked there, but was fired. And Peabody confirmed all of this. This would all indicate J and J still is a working mine, but one that's in the process of shutting down."

George kicked a stone to the side of the road and shook his head at the ground. "I don't have all the answers! Mike, if you, Jane, and Beth can get up there tomorrow, I think your visit might get a lot of our questions answered. If they are closing and pulling out, you'd better get up there soon. That is, if you hope to save Peter."

## TWELVE

Just then a battered pickup truck pulled up and two characters climbed out. "Hey, George, you got a lost truck driver?" asked a barrel-chested mountain of a man of about 30.

"No, Moose. This is Jake and he's not lost at all. He just got back from Slippery Gulch."

I shook hands with Moose watching my hand almost completely disappear in his. Looking at my truck he asked in total amazement, "In that?"

"Yeah," George said. "He had to go in to pick up a load."

"You've got more balls than I've got," Moose said. "I was in there a couple of years ago in this truck of mine and I don't mind telling you I was mighty nervous going across that cliff."

"That wasn't one of my more pleasant experiences driving," I said, "but it'll give me something to talk about for a long time. In fact, when I left here this morning, I had dark brown hair." At 57, my hair was, as they say, "a distinguished silver."

Everybody cracked up on that one.

Moose was several inches over 6-foot-5 if he was an inch. He carried some 300 pounds and was solid muscle. He had shoulder length, dark brown hair, brown eyes, and a full beard. He wore work boots, jeans, and a plaid shirt. He could have passed as Paul Bunyan's baby brother. Although he looked big and tough enough to play an offensive lineman for any team in the NFL, I was assured he was Basin's gentle giant. I learned that he and his friend worked on a highway crew for the state of Montana. "Twig" was about 5-foot-4, 160 pounds, with short blond hair, blue eyes, and a clean-shaven face.

I shook hands with Twig and said, "By any chance, your name wouldn't be Forrest, would it?"

"Yeah," he said. "How did you guess that?"

"I have a friend named Forrest who is also nicknamed Twig. I'm not sure if I have the story quite right, but after he was born, an uncle or other relative said something to the effect: He's too small to be a forest. Let's call him Twig, and Twig it was. Back in the '80s he moved out of the area, and once he relocated, he sent me a letter. However, the whole top of the envelope had gotten wet and his address was smudged. Even the postmark! He put no address in his letter, so I could never write him back."

"That's too bad. But you're right: That's about how I got my nickname too."

After the introductions and small talk, George said, "Let's go inside for a minute."

We followed him, but Twig went and looked at the truck one last time, turned, and asked, "You really drove that thing into Slippery Gulch?"

"Yeah, I did but I'd never do it again. Going in wasn't so bad, but coming out was a cliffhanger. I could see over the edge. My tires were right there too. By the time I got across, I was sweating like a pig."

"Have you ever thought you may have a guardian angel?" Twig asked.

Nobody laughed. "As a matter of fact, more than once! But after that trip, I'd sure like to meet him."

Once we got inside, Moose and Twig ordered beers all around. "I'd love one, but I've got to drive tonight," I replied.

"You can sure tell this guy isn't from around here," Moose said to no one in particular. "He has good manners."

They laughed as we sat down. Jane delivered the beers and took a seat. Then George asked, "Moose, Twig? You've both been up there in the past 5 or 6 years, haven't you?" They both answered yes. "Well, have either one of you seen anything odd about the place?"

With a questioning look Twig said no, but Moose asked, "What do you mean by odd?"

Mike answered, "Well, you know, strange, like maybe something you saw that you knew couldn't be but was. And you couldn't explain it."

Moose sat deep in thought staring at his beer mug as we all watched quietly. Then he just took another sip of beer. I think we all knew now he'd seen something, but what? None of us said a word.

Finally, he looked at me. Then at the others. "Do any of you know Dirk Jenson from Wickes?" They all nodded yes.

"You're all going to think I'm nuts."

"Twig might," Jane said, "but I've got a feeling the rest of us won't. What was it, Moose?"

"Two years ago this October, Dirk and me decided to try the woods behind Slippery Gulch for bear. We decided since it's so hard to get into it probably hasn't been hunted in years. The snow came late to the high country that year. We were able to drive all the way into town. The snow in town had been protected by the buildings but the cliff was dry.

"We got there about nine in the morning. We parked right in front of the old Jacob's Mercantile. We grabbed what we needed and took off for the woods. We were in the woods all day and never saw so much as a track—well, that is until we got back to the truck."

Mike interrupted, "Let me guess, you saw tracks and they weren't bear."

Moose looked at Mike in wide-eyed shock. "Sounds like you've been there, done that."

"Keep going, Moose," Jane urged.

"When I parked the truck, I parked in the middle of the snow. It was only a couple of inches deep. When we got back, as we approached the truck, we both noticed tracks going right up to the driver's door but none leading away. I thought somebody was in my truck. I opened the door sudden like. Then we checked behind the seat. There wasn't anyone."

"Where did the tracks come from?" Mike asked.

"Looked like they came from between two buildings but when we followed them backwards, out of the snow, they disappeared in the dirt in front of a building. They just... started...out of nowhere," Moose said.

"And that's it?" George smirked.

"Well that's enough, isn't it?" Moose shot back.

I looked over at Twig. He was looking at his friend as if he was crazy.

"No, it's not," Mike said. "For instance, how big were the tracks?"

"Well, they were a child's tracks," Moose confessed to Mike, with amazement on his face.

"And what else was unusual about those tracks, Moose?" Mike asked.

"You're not going to believe this, but the kid who made them must have been barefoot. Look, somehow I get the feeling all of you know what I'm talking about."

"Yeah," Mike said, "I saw tracks of a small child, too, but Jake not only saw the tracks, he saw the child. Talked to him too! And George here talked to him on Jake's cell phone. Jake, why don't you pick it up from here?"

"First of all, Mike, I saw a child but I don't believe he was the child who made those tracks." I related my entire experience to Moose and Twig from the time I first entered the town until I left, taking a picture on the hill overlooking the town. I mentioned everything I thought they would be most interested in—the forklift, my pen, cell phone, and camera. I also told them a lone horse loaded the crusher. And there was no sign of any kind of machinery, just that crazy tripod.

Moose and Twig were totally engrossed. When I had finished relating my experience, Jane said, "You took several pictures of Peter but did you take any of Peabody?"

"No, I'm sorry to say, I didn't. He was quite a character but I never thought about the camera until after I'd left his company and ran into Peter again."

"Does anyone have any idea what's going on up there?" Twig asked.

"I have a theory," George said and then related it to Moose and Twig.

"Sounds reasonable," Twig sighed, "But what about the footprints?"

Moose nodded in agreement. I asked Mike, "You never went back, did you? And in fact, after you saw them, you left rather quickly, didn't you?" Moose kind of chuckled and Mike got a little red in the face and reluctantly agreed. Then I looked at Moose and asked, "Moose, have you been back since you saw the prints?"

Hesitantly his smile dropped, "Well, no."

"Do you know if Dirk has?"

"Not that I know of," he said.

"Would I be wrong in guessing that both you and Dirk also departed rather quickly?"

"Well, let's say we didn't waste much time. Can you blame us?" asked Moose defensively.

"No, I can't," I admitted.

Jane started to chuckle. "But you didn't, Jake. Yet these two big, brave outdoorsmen took off like dogs with their tails between their legs."

"Wait a minute, Jane," I said. "For one thing, this morning when Mike was telling me about the tracks, I thought you guys were trying to spook me out with ghost town talk. But I didn't see unexplained tracks. The tracks I saw I could account for. I don't know what I would have done if I had seen detached tracks. And then stopping like that with no one in them! If your cult idea is right, George, they're sure scaring the tar out of a few people, don't you think?"

"I hate to admit it, but I guess it was pretty effective," Mike said. "But then why did you see all those people, Jake?"

"You've got to remember, Mike, Peabody got a hold of my company and asked for a truck to come in and pick up that crusher. Probably everybody in town knew that a truck was coming in that day, so folks were there to make it appear natural. But Peter was there to warn me to be careful. He was not part of any orchestrated plan."

"How do you explain the tracks, Jake?" Moose asked.

"I can't. You guys are better outdoorsmen than I am. Mike said earlier there'd be a way of obliterating them."

"That's true," Moose said, "but a cult?"

"Hey, this whole thing is just a theory. Does anybody else have any other ideas?" George asked.

We all sat there looking at each other not saying a word until Twig jumped. "Yeah, I've got one. It's a ghost town!" We all nodded in Twig's direction with smirks on our faces. "Maybe Jake's a ghost too," Twig added reaching for a laugh that would relieve the tension.

"Shoot, I've been discovered," and I yelled boo and jumped at all of them.

That did it. They all jumped a little and were amused. Jane asked, "Who's ready for another beer?"

Later when she brought the beer for everyone but me, I said, "Don't you think a ghost can hold a can?"

Jane turned serious. "You know, if George's theory is right, and so far it's the best one I've heard tonight, we've got to get up to Slippery Gulch first thing in the morning and find that kid. If they leave, we'll never find him. Lord knows what will become of him then."

"Yeah, you're right, Jane," Mike said. "You'd better call Beth right away."

Jane said, "Jake, I know you've got to get going, but could you wait 10 more minutes? Beth will probably want to talk to you."

"Who's Beth?" Twig asked.

As Jane and I stood up to go to the office, George said, "Beth Jackson, the county social worker."

Jane called her office and caught Beth just as she was leaving. Jane apologized and asked if she could spare a few minutes. Then Jane explained she thought she had a desperate child abuse and neglect case, and time was of the essence. She told who I was and that I could explain the situation better than she could. She then handed the phone to me.

I introduced myself, described Peter's physical appearance, quoted our conversations, and pointed out the obvious fear Peter had for his father. I explained how he devoured my cookies so fast I had to slow him down. I explained the reaction Peabody had when I told him I'd been talking to Peter. Beth asked a few questions, and then I handed the phone back to Jane.

Jane went on to explain our theory of the cult and how we suspected they were getting ready to move, making it too late to rescue Peter. Apparently Beth agreed, for she wanted to meet Jane, Mike, and George in Basin the next morning. When Jane hung up, she said Beth would have a sheriff's deputy in tow as they went up to Slippery Gulch in a group.

Both Moose and Twig said they'd like to go too but had to work. George had to work also. At that point I stood and said I'd like to go myself, but I had business in Reno. I thanked all of them for the help they'd been and especially thanked Jane for the interest she took in Peter and for her kind hospitality. I offered again to pay for my dinner, but she and George wouldn't hear of it. I wished them luck the next day and told them to be sure to say hello to Peter for me. They assured me they would, and with that, I headed for the door, all following me as though I were family.

Outside, I promised to call in the next few days to see how everything went. Jane, Mike, and I exchanged addresses and promised to keep in touch. I also told them I would try and get up here again; but with my schedule, Lord only knew when. They understood.

When we got out to my tractor door, both Moose and Twig (who had their CDLs, or commercial driver's licenses, because of driving state construction trucks) wanted to look inside. Both were surprised to see it was an automatic and started asking a lot of questions. I answered their questions and I went around, shaking hands with all the guys. Then I came to Jane. "Jane, you know Peter is really a filthy mess. When you get him back here, would you mind throwing him in the tub for a good soaking? He could really use it."

"Way ahead of you, Jake. Based on your description of him, I already thought about that. Don't worry, when I get finished with him, he'll shine." She then gave me a big hug and a bigger smile and said, "Thanks for caring, Jake, and keep in touch." I promised I would, climbed in, started the Babes, and took off for Reno, giving one final blast on the air horn to my five new friends getting smaller in my rearview mirror.

## THIRTEEN

It would have been nice to make a couple of hundred miles that night, but I didn't leave until about nine my time. So I stopped at a small truck stop in Dillon, about 75 miles south of Basin. I'd had a hard, nerve-racking, emotional day and I was beat, so I parked and went to bed.

About midnight, there was a knock on my door. I walked up to the driver's seat, not really awake, and looked down into the eyes of a Lot Lizard. She was a relatively attractive young woman of about 20 with dark brown hair and eyes, wearing a loose-fitting T-shirt and tight jeans. She was rather well endowed, so as I looked down I got quite a view.

As I rolled down my window, she said, "Would you like some company?" in a sexy voice.

"Not particularly," I said. "Would you?"

"Oh yeah, I'd love some company, honey."

"Well, okay" I said, looking at my passenger seat. "Why don't you go to the other side of my truck. You can sit in the passenger seat and I'll listen to your problems for a half an hour and charge you only 50 dollars."

"What? You expect me to pay you?"

"Lady, I've got a degree in psychology. Any young woman wandering around a dark truck stop looking for sex in this age of HIV, AIDS, and other sexually transmitted diseases, obviously needs all the help she can get."

Based on what she said to me, I kind of assumed she didn't want any help. As she walked away, she turned around and let me know she thought I was "number one." I went back to bed, chuckling to myself, but wondered if she might have been raised in some sort of cult. I fell asleep praying they'd find my pathetic little man in time.

The next day I was up by five, grabbed a cup of coffee, and took off. This would be a beautiful and interesting trip, historically. I wanted to occupy my mind with something as rock-solid as my steering wheel just to clear my head of cult and ghost theories—with all due respect to my new friends.

First of all, just to the west of Dillon about 35 miles is the town of Bannack, the first capital of the territory of Montana and the site of Montana's first gold strike in 1862. Although the town is a state park, it had not been commercialized the way Virginia City and Nevada City were. Not only that, the Lewis and Clark Trail went right through Dillon. (I guess a better way of putting it would be to say Dillon sits on the Lewis and Clark Trail.)

To the west of Dillon is the Bitterroot Range. This was the range that almost wiped out the Lewis and Clark Expedition. It possibly would have if it hadn't had been for Sacagawea, the Shoshone Indian girl captured by the Mandan Indians while raiding the Shoshones several years earlier. As a young teenager, she was pregnant. Her husband was the French–Canadian trapper Toussaint Charbonneau. The Mandans lived far to the east of Butte in what is now North Dakota.

They were interesting in their own right. Many had gray eyes and auburn hair. One of their many legends states that at one time a flood covered the entire earth, and humans and animals were saved from drowning by a huge canoe. After a great many days of rain a dove was sent out to find land. They also told of the son of the Great Spirit who was sent to earth to live but was killed. However, no one had remembered his name. I thought of the Bible stories I'd grown up with, for there were obvious echoes in Mandan lore. I found my mind drifting back to another's boyhood. Would cult parents name a boy after the famous St. Peter of the scriptures? I doubt it.

Another legend stated that they had come to this land from far away. They crossed a very large lake in many large ships at least 1,000 years ago. Because many of the words they spoke appeared to have a Welsh origin, Clark speculated they might have come from Wales. Interesting, but I guess we'll never know for sure. The entire tribe was wiped out by white man's disease in the 1830s. (Could there be a ghost still around able to play with the minds of unsuspecting truckers like me?)

Lewis and Clark spent the winter with the Mandans and by spring Sacagawea was the mother of an infant boy, who she named Pompey. When it was time for the expedition to move on in the spring of 1805, it had three additional members— Sacagawea, her husband, and her infant son.

If it hadn't been for Sacagawea, it's very possible the expedition would have perished in the Bitter Roots. This was on my mind as I pulled into a truck stop in Idaho Falls for breakfast.

First, I punched into my computer asking for directions to Smith and Associates in Reno. While waiting for my answer, I brought my logbook up to date. Shortly I got my answer: "No directions available." So I sent in a message asking for the phone number. Again after about 3 minutes, I got a message saying "No phone number available." All I could think of was, here we go again.

The good thing was, Reno was no Slippery Gulch. At least I could find Reno and once I got there I could look up Smith and Associates in the phone book, call, and get directions.

Meanwhile the thought of scrambled eggs, toast, and coffee drew me inside.

# FOURTEEN

It was almost 10:00 my time, close to 8:00 Basin time, when I assumed
Jane, Mike, Beth, and the deputy sheriff would be closing in on
Slippery Gulch. I wouldn't find out until later that day what
they found. It developed that upon reaching the section of the
road that crosses the 200 yards of cliff, they stopped and Mike
called George on his cell phone. They related the following
conversation to me:

"George, this is Mike."

"You there already?"

"No, we're at the cliff. Look, we have a little problem. Is
there any chance you could come out here?"

"I'm kind of deep into my bookkeeping for my July estimated taxes, but what seems to be the problem?"

"There's been a landslide. About 20 feet of the road is gone."

"What do you mean, gone?"

"When dirt and rock slid down the mountainside and went
over the cliff, it took 20 feet of the road with it. The road is now
about 4 feet wide. The section closest to the cliff broke off and
went over the edge. In other words, the cliff moved back about
4 feet."

"Oh you're kidding! It must have been the weight of Jake's
truck that brought it down. It looks like Jake was really lucky. If
that would have let loose when Jake—"

"I don't think so, George," Mike cut in. "Jake's tire tracks go
right up and into the slide area. You can also see where he got
out of the truck and walked into the slide area just as he said,

then walked back to his truck. I'm not sure but I think the landslide happened before Jake ever got to it. There are signs of a small stream that had run down the middle of it. That's why I want you to take a look at this."

"Mike, you're not making any sense. If the slide would have happened before Jake got to it, there's obviously no way Jake could have gotten into Slippery Gulch. Do you think everything Jake told us was a lie?"

"No, not at all, George, but I really don't know what to think. Jane and I are really at a loss. Beth and the deputy were upset about being pulled out on a wild goose chase. They were ready to leave until we saw Jake's tracks continuing on the other side. I don't want to tell you any more, George. I'd like you to come out here and draw your own conclusions."

"I'll be right up." And with that George hung up.

About 15 minutes later George pulled up behind the other two vehicles. He walked up to the others who were all standing within five feet of the slide area. He stood there studying the ground and finally said, "This doesn't make any sense. We haven't had enough rain for months to cause this kind of slide. This has to be a result of the spring melt, which means it happened in either March or April yet those are clearly Jake's tracks on the other side. I have to get into town." Walking back to his truck he soon returned with a rope. Tying one end to the front bumper of Mike's 4-by-4, he tied the other end around his waist. He then started across. With each step he checked for firmness. He also checked the ground for cracks, which may indicate the rest could go, but saw none. The ground seemed to be solid. Once on the other side he looked back to the others. "I'm walking into town. Anybody want to come along?"

The rest of them looked at each other and started to walk toward George. Together they looked at the signs of weathering and erosion as they walked along. Once on the other side, they could all clearly see the signs of my truck.

Ray, the deputy sheriff, said, "George, this is illogical. Even I can see the slide happened during the spring melt, yet his tracks are clearly on this side of the slide. The best practical joker in the world couldn't do this. What's going on?"

"I don't know," George said. "Moose drove into Slippery Gulch last November so we know the road was open then. Let's keep walking and see what we find."

They continued on and saw at the top of the hill where I had taken my last picture of the town. They walked down the hill and into town and soon came to the place where I climbed out of my truck and took my pictures of Peter. What they didn't see though disturbed them greatly. They knew then they had to see my pictures when they were developed.

## FIFTEEN

Meanwhile, I continued my trip south having no idea what was going on in Slippery Gulch. June 30 was a beautiful, clear day and as I approached Idaho Falls, I was able to look east to my left and see the Grand Teton Mountains, one of the most beautiful mountain ranges in North America. A French mountain man named the range in the late 1700s. As the story goes, the old mountain man was perhaps out on his own a little too long, and when he first set eyes on the two major peaks, they reminded him of a particular part of a woman's anatomy, thus the Grand Tetons. Lord only knows if the legend is true.

Continuing south on I-15, I passed through the cities of Blackfoot and Pocatello. Near Blackfoot are the reconstructed remains of Fort Hall, the first signs of civilization for the Oregon Trail travelers since leaving Fort Laramie in what is now Wyoming. Looking at the map, it doesn't look like much. Today a trucker can make it in a day without pushing it. But 150 years ago, averaging 10 to 15 miles a day—maybe 20 on a good day—it was a whole different story. On some other days it was zero, what with a broken axle, a death, a breakout of illness, or Indian attacks.

Sixty miles south of Pocatello, I crossed into Utah. At about mile marker 369 is the exit for the town of Promontory, the point where east first met west over the railroad tracks of America. South of there one goes through the cities of Ogden and finally Salt Lake City.

Although the famous mountain man Jim Bridger first discovered Salt Lake, he did not recognize it for what it was. From where he stood, he could not see across it. And since it was salt water, he assumed he'd found a short cut to the Pacific Ocean. It wasn't until several years later that another famous mountain man, Jedediah Smith, came upon Salt Lake and proceeded to walk around it, proving once and for all that it was a lake.

In 1847 Brigham Young and the Mormons moved in; however, they were not the first white settlers to live in the area. Miles Goodyear had a farm about 40 miles away in Ogden's Hole. The neighbors were getting too close for comfort and through mutual agreement, the Mormons bought him out. Goodyear moved on to enjoy his privacy again.

I stopped at the terminal to say hello to some friends and then headed for I-80 and Reno. From Salt Lake I-80 runs along the southern edge of the lake and out into the Bonneville Salt Flats and a whole lot of desert, for the most part, all the way to Reno. However, there are a lot of neat little towns along the way, such as Elko, Battle Mountain, and Winnemucca. Near Wells, Nevada, I passed through a corner of the Humboldt National Forest. As a native of the Northeastern hardwood forest, the Humboldt Forest looked like a field of shrubs.

## SIXTEEN

As I approached Reno, I pulled into a TA truck stop in Sparks, a suburb of Reno. The Truck Stops of America (TA) is a quality nationwide chain that provides all the services a driver could want. I decided to check out the large wall map of Reno for Donner Road. Strange, but it was not listed in the Reno glossary of roads. Donner Terrace was but no Donner Road. On the map Donner Terrace appeared to be quite short.

I walked to the fuel desk and asked the woman behind the counter if she knew where Donner Road was in Reno. "I've heard of a Donner Terrace but not Donner Road but I think Donner Terrace is residential. That's not what you're looking for, is it?" she said.

"No. My computer and my bill of lading both say Donner Road."

"There are a lot of new industrial areas springing up all over the city. Maybe it's one of them. What's the name of the place you're looking for?"

I told her and she asked if I had a phone number. When I said no, she grabbed a Reno phone book and looked it up. But it wasn't listed. Now why didn't that surprise me?

She said, "Why don't you call the Reno police? They should be able to help." I thought, well, here we go again. I thanked her and walked back to the wall of pay phones and dialed.

The individual who answered sounded like a young woman, perhaps in her twenties. I explained who I was, what I was looking for and why. I explained that I knew there was a Donner Terrace that is residential yet both my computer and the bill of lading stated the address as 702 Donner Road. She put me on hold for a minute. When she came back, she said she was going to transfer me to an individual more familiar with the city of Reno.

I'd been sitting on hold for several minutes when a Sergeant Rodriguez came on the line. I again explained who I was, what I was trying to find and why.

"Are you sure you have a load going to Smith and Associates?"

At this point, I was a little put out. I said, "Of course I'm sure. The name and address of the firm are in my computer and on the bill of lading."

"What are you hauling?"

"A 2-ton crusher."

"Where are you calling from?"

I told him and then asked, "Would you mind telling me what's going on?"

"To be perfectly honest," he said, "I don't know."

"Well, why don't you give it your best shot."

He ignored my request and asked me who I drove for and exactly where I was parked in the huge lot. I told him and he said, "Stay by your truck. I'll be there in about half an hour."

"Couldn't you at least give me a hint as to what you think might be going on?"

His only response was, "Just stay by your truck."

"Wait a minute. It's almost 7:00 my time and I haven't had breakfast yet. Would you mind if we meet in the restaurant? I've got gray hair and a beard. I'll be sitting alone and reading a book. I'll treat you to a cup of coffee."

"Well, okay, I'll see you when I get there." As I walked out to my truck, thinking about the situation I was in, I was at a complete loss. There was no Donner Road, and why was he so surprised I was delivering to a Smith and Associates?

I grabbed my book—a good mystery—and my bills at the same time and walked back into the building and called my driver manager from a table phone in the restaurant. I ordered a cup of coffee and sat there on hold for a few minutes. I finally got the night DM. My regular DM didn't start until 6:00 Mountain time. As a cross-country truck driver, time can be a little confusing at times. Because of the logbook, I have to stay on Eastern time. So it was 7:00 my time, 4:00 where I was calling from, and 5:00 where I was calling to. I asked her to confirm the name and address of the consignee, which she did, and there was nothing new. I explained the situation I found myself in, and she just said, "Keep me posted." I said okay and hung up.

About an hour or so later, two police officers walked in, one from Reno and one from Sparks. Immediately behind them walked in two more. As they got closer, I could see they were the Nevada Department of Transportation. I thought to myself, good grief, what's next, the FBI? Little did I know the FBI was not far behind.

The first police officer was from Reno. He had sergeant stripes on his sleeve. I could see his name tag read Rodriguez so I stood up and introduced myself. Hispanic, he was probably in his early sixties, and had a full head of gray hair. He was about 6-foot tall and average weight, but built more like a 35-year-old.

He introduced me to the Sparks police officer, Corporal Jantz a 20-something kid who was the best-looking police officer I'd ever seen. She was about 5-foot-2 with eyes of blue. Her long auburn hair and figure could have knocked my socks off. I certainly could understand why the sergeant knew this Sparks police officer. He did not introduce me to the DOT men at that time, which didn't bother me. I couldn't figure why they were there anyway.

None of us were smiling, and I figured I had the best reason not to be. Every trucker in the restaurant was looking at me, all undoubtedly wondering what was going on and what I had done. Of course, I was basically wondering the same thing

After the introductions, I got the ball rolling. "Gentlemen, have a seat. I promised to treat the sergeant to coffee so it's my treat. I just wasn't expecting a party. So, sergeant, what gives?"

"Sorry for getting here a little later than I said, but I had to let the Sparks police know what was going on. I also took time to look something up."

"That's okay. I called my company just to make sure the name and address of the consignee I have is the same one they have, and it is. Now if you don't mind filling me in, what is going on?"

"May I see your bill of lading?" Rodriguez asked.

"Sure, no problem." I opened the trip envelope and produced the bills and the seal manifest, and handed them to the sergeant. The two DOT officers looked at them. "This is what you were given at J and J Mines?" a heavyset DOT officer asked.

"Yes, sir, that's it. He wrote both out by hand."

"Why didn't he at least make copies of it?" the sergeant asked.

"He did have a copy for himself, but it looked as if he wrote both out by hand. It didn't even look as if carbon paper was used. This was the strangest place I've ever been. There was no office machinery of any type. In fact, I saw no signs of electricity anyplace at the mine, or for that matter, in the town. But from what I can see, the bills are legal, aren't they?"

"Yes, they're legal, just different. I've never seen bills like this before," said the heavyset DOT man. "They're like something out of the 1800s."

"Tell me about it." It suddenly occurred to me that perhaps the reason why the sergeant didn't introduce the DOT men was because he didn't know their names. They were both wearing Nevada DOT jackets, which covered their name tags. I took it upon myself to do the introductions.

I looked at the heavyset DOT man and said, "By the way, I'm Jake Winters," and stuck out my hand.

He took my hand and said, "I'm Rafael Sanchez and this is Tom Dooley."

I shook his hand but before I could make a wisecrack, Mr. Dooley said, "And I don't hang down my head." We both chuckled but I wasn't sure if the younger people among us got the joke. The little exchange served to relieve any embarrassment the sergeant may have had for not making the introductions himself.

Mr. Sanchez was a middle-aged Hispanic with brown eyes and black balding hair on top when he removed his hat to wipe perspiration from his damp scalp. He was weathered from years of legwork on the road. No bureaucrat, he!

The younger Mr. Dooley enjoyed a full head of blond hair. I saw behind his blue sunglasses that helped hide his baby face. He smiled easily. He was the type I could swap one-liners with and not be out of place with respect to the business at hand.

Sanchez asked, "Who made out this bill of lading?"

"The owner of the mine, Jeremiah Peabody."

"Did he load the truck or was it someone else?" Dooley asked.

"Peabody and his horse loaded the truck." They all looked at each other. "In fact, here's another strange thing about the place: I never saw any machinery of any type and I never once saw or heard another employee of the mine the entire time I was there."

"What do you mean, Peabody and his horse?" Dooley asked.

I explained the loading process and drew on a napkin the mechanism that was used.

"Good grief," Dooley said. "That's like something right out of the Dark Ages."

"Yeah, I know. Look, would you mind filling me in? I think it's time."

They all looked at Rodriguez and he looked at me, appearing not to know quite where to start. "According to your bills, you clearly picked up this load at J and J Mines in Slippery Gulch, Montana. There's no problem there, but you're delivering the load to Smith and Associates at 702 Donner Road in Reno, and that is a problem."

"There used to be a Donner Road in Reno, but it is now buried under I-80, which runs through the city."

I sat there listening with great interest. He continued, "As I mentioned, I found something before coming over here. I have a book on the history of Reno and I thought I remembered seeing something in there several years ago, so I checked it out and I was right. I found a picture of the Smith and Associates building. It was located at 702 Donner Road."

"Was?" I asked.

"That's right. They went bankrupt in 1901 and never re-opened. As I said, Donner Road no longer exists."

"Now wait a minute sergeant, what you're telling me makes no sense. I have a crusher shipped by Peabody at J and J Mines to an address that hasn't existed for years, and to a consignee that's been out of business for 100 years? That's illogical." I decided not to mention the letter but wasn't sure why.

At that point Sanchez said, "Now that you mention the crusher, why don't we take a look at it?"

"Well, as long as you sign both the bill of lading and the seal manifest, and identify yourself, including badge number, and you indicate that you're the one who removed the seal!" I said.

"No problem," he said and did as I requested.

We all finished our coffee and walked out to the truck. I grabbed my gloves and a small tool to easily break the seal, then we all headed for the back of the trailer. I then handed the tool to Sanchez and said, "Here, you just signed for the privilege. You do it."

He took the tool and easily broke the seal. Then he took it and compared the number on the seal with the number on the seal manifest. They matched. I then put my gloves on, opened the right door and walked it around to the side to latch it. I heard Sanchez say, "What are you trying to prove?"

"Excuse me?" I said and looked into the back of the trailer. The 2-by-4s were secure right where I'd nailed them to the floor, and the rope was still there, but the crusher was gone. I was as dumbfounded as anyone was. I was the driver and I was responsible for the load; suspicion immediately fell on me.

"Where is it?" Sanchez asked.

I couldn't speak at first. Things like this aren't supposed to happen. Trucks are hijacked, trailers are stolen, trailers are broken into and loads are stolen; but who could steal a 2-ton crusher without breaking the seal and opening the doors? Still not answering, I crawled under the trailer to examine the underside of the floor. Sanchez, suddenly realizing what I was doing, crawled under with me. Everything was intact, as expected.

At that point, I turned to Sanchez and said, "Sir, I really have no idea where the crusher is or how this could happen." I could see by the look on his face that, not only did he believe me, but he was as baffled as I was.

The two of us crawled out from under the trailer. Sanchez said something to Dooley and he walked back to his car. Sanchez looked over the bill of lading again, and the rest of us stood around doing nothing. Finally, after about 20 minutes, I asked, "Are we waiting for something?" As if on cue two plain "black wrappers"—black unmarked police cars—pulled up. I thought, "Why do they need so many DOT guys?" As it turned out, they weren't DOT. They were FBI. Things were heating up, I was outnumbered, and it wasn't looking too good for good old number one. Sometimes I don't think I get paid enough and this was one of those times.

Although there were four of them, there was only one I really noticed. Trim, in great shape physically, and not wearing any rings. It so happens I have a weakness for long red hair and blue eyes. Her one deficit was cosmetic. She wore large, orangish, plastic-rimmed glasses that clashed terribly with her red hair. She put me in mind of a circus clown impersonating an FBI agent for the laughs. But I was not laughing!

They each introduced themselves in mumbles, quickly flashing thin identification. She was Special Agent Smith, but she didn't say much. Questioning was left up to Special Agent Watson.

Watson was a homely man—nose far too big for his face, thick lips, and full black eyebrows. Gray in his hair made his mane lighter than his eyebrows. He had to be 6-foot-4. His appearance was unusual, strange. He looked like a scientific experiment that failed. Nevertheless, he was all FBI.

Watson instructed me to drive my truck down to the city impound yard and leave it until they finished their investigation.

I announced to all that before I went anywhere, I had two phone calls to make.

"To whom?" Watson asked.

"The first one is to my company. This is their truck and before I move it anywhere, I have to let them know why. I think they will want to talk to you, too."

"And who's the second call to?" Watson asked.

"PTLA, my legal representative as a professional driver."

"I don't really think that's necessary, Mr. Winters," Watson said.

"Remember Waco? Remember Ruby Ridge? I'm sorry, sir, but I think it is." I don't know where that courage came from, but I got my way.

Sergeant Rodriguez, Sanchez, Watson, and I huddled around my truck while I called my driver manager. By this time, Jason, my regular DM, was in. I explained my situation briefly. He was dumbfounded. I was transferred to his supervisor with the same results. I was then transferred to a vice president in charge of load planning. I once again sketched my story. I could tell he either didn't believe me or didn't understand. More than likely it was a little bit of both.

"Mr. Resnec, there's someone here you need to talk to. I'm going to put Special Agent Watson from the FBI on the phone."

Before I handed the phone over to "Lurch," I heard Resnec say, "Who?" I handed the phone to Watson.

"Mr. Resnec, I'm Special Agent Watson from the FBI. I'm investigating the disappearance of a 2-ton crusher from one of your trailers."

There was a short pause and Watson said, "No, sir, I'm not kidding." Another pause. "You have to realize, Mr. Resnec, we have not officially started the investigation, so I'm unable to answer your question. Our first priority is to secure the trailer, then go over it with a fine-tooth comb. And of course, we have a lot of questions for your driver."

"I'm sorry, sir, I can't answer that at this time."

"According to both the Reno and Sparks police and the Nevada DOT, the seal was intact."

"No, there is no sign of forced entry, but we have to impound the trailer and do a thorough inspection."

"I really can't say how long it will take."

"Yes, I'll keep in touch." Lurch—er, Watson—wrote down a number and hung up.

"One more call to make," I said.

I started to dial when Lurch said, "We've got to get this truck to the impound yard. You can call from down there. Now get in that truck and follow me."

"No," I said still not sure where this newfound courage was coming from. "I'm not under arrest and I'm calling from here." I continued dialing.

After a couple of minutes on hold, I got through to a representative. I went through my story, as best I could, explaining my present situation. I gave him the location of the inbound lot, and where I'd be with the FBI. John, the individual representing the PTLA, told me that as long as he's been doing this he has never even heard of anything like this. He also told me not to answer any questions without an attorney present. I asked when he thought that would be. "Within a couple of hours," I was told. He asked for the phone number of where I'd be. I got that information from Lurch and passed it along. John wished me luck, told me to hold tight, and hung up. I was now on my own, at least for a while.

# SEVENTEEN

I disconnected the line and said to Lurch, "Okay, let's go."

I climbed into my truck and we headed for the impound yard in downtown Reno, with my personal police escort. After locking my tractor, I got a ride with Lurch and the redhead to the FBI offices on Kietzke Lane. I was asked a couple of questions by Lurch but told him I would not answer them without an attorney present. However, I told them again that my only involvement with the load was picking it up at the mine. I added that upon reaching Reno, the seal was still intact.

As if Lurch didn't hear a thing I said, he asked, "How did you get it out of the truck?"

I wanted to say, "What part of 'my only involvement' don't you understand?" Instead, I said, "I'll wait for an attorney." That silenced the car.

When we got to the federal building, we rode the elevator to the third floor and walked into a small FBI reception area. I was instructed to have a seat in one of the two chairs. Lurch disappeared into one of the back offices, which was a relief.

Ten minutes later, a man walked in, apparently just back from fishing. He looked around and walked up to me and said, "Are you Jake Winters?"

"Yes," I said and stuck out my hand. He took my hand as he introduced himself as Frank Krandell, a federal attorney representing Krandell and Grimes. He had the peaceful manner of a fisherman. He was pleasant looking, a far cry from Lurch. His handshake was firm and confident.

"You were fishing?" I asked.

"Yeah. The trout in the Truckee River present a real challenge."

"Gee, I'm sorry I pulled you out of the river, Mr. Krandell."

"Call me Frank and don't be. This case sounded too interesting to pass up. Now let's find a private place where we can talk."

They gave us a storage-size consulting room with two chairs and a small table. After getting situated, Frank took out a tablet and asked me to start at the beginning.

I started right back in Butte, Montana, at the time of dispatch, and the problems I had in finding the town of Slippery Gulch. I found it only after talking to a sheriff in Butte. I mentioned how he gave me the phone of the sheriff in Jefferson County, and how he gave the number of the Silver Dollar Saloon in Basin where I finally met George, Jane, and Mike. He asked me for their phone numbers. I told him about the drive in, the drive out, and literally everything in between. I also mentioned George's cult theory, which he found interesting.

I went over the loading process in great detail and he found that fascinating. "So it appeared to you as if he'd never heard of a forklift?" Frank asked.

"Yes!"

"That is really strange. Even a survivalist cult leader was not a cult leader from his youth. And the ballpoint pen: That just doesn't make sense. Now I can understand a 6-year-old boy being born in a situation like that and never hearing of a telephone, but Peabody....And the boy gave you no details as to how his father was going to get even?"

"No, he was scared to death of being caught by his father. He ran away before I could learn anything else."

Many more questions were asked and answered. Finally Frank said, "Maybe the disappearance of the crusher does have something to do with the boy's father. But then again, maybe not. I think it's time to look at the trailer."

The two of us got up and walked to the front desk and asked for Lurch—sorry, Watson.

A few minutes later, he came out and Frank informed him that we wanted to look at the trailer. Watson told him where it was and we both headed for the door when Lurch said, "Winters stays here."

Frank turned around and said, "Oh, I wasn't aware my client was under arrest." Watson didn't say anything but just stood there. Frank said, "Well, is he or isn't he?"

There came a "no."

"I'm glad you said that, agent," Frank said. "In fact, you don't even have a cause to hold him, do you?" I liked this guy.

"No, not as yet, but the lab boys are going over the trailer right now. It shouldn't be long. If Winters goes, I want one of my agents to go along."

"Fine," said Frank. "He can drive."

"She," said Lurch. "Her name is Agent Smith." I smiled.

A few minutes later, a comical Agent Smith came out to the front counter. Maybe she was color-blind. I was going to introduce them to one another but quickly realized they had already met. We walked out to the standard-issue black sedan and drove to the impound yard, saying nothing. As we pulled into the yard, I saw an individual climbing out of my tractor and I went nuts: "Hey, what the heck are they doing in my truck? They have no business in there."

Right away Smith said, "Do you have something to hide, Mr. Winters?"

"Yeah, I have a 4,000-pound crusher stuffed under my bunk. Look, I don't have a thing to hide, but I don't appreciate strangers going through my house."

"First of all, Mr. Winters, that is not a house, it's just a truck." Smith said. "And two, we, as the FBI, have a job to do."

Frank tried to cool me down but after Smith's last statement, it was too late. "First of all, Ms. Smith, I'm on the road two to three months at a time. When I leave home that 'truck' becomes my house. Now I'm sure you wouldn't admit it, being FBI, but I really doubt if you would appreciate strangers going through your house either. I've heard the stories around the country of the FBI planting illegal items to trap unsuspecting citizens, and I'm one of a growing number of individuals in the country who don't trust the FBI any further than I can throw them. Second, Ms. Smith, I'm fully aware of the fact that the FBI would love to have unlimited access to my property but there is something called the Constitution."

There was about thirty seconds of cold silence in the car, during which Frank took my arm and was about to say something when Smith said, "Mr. Winters, I apologize. I don't know much about the trucking industry. I thought you men were on the road for five or six days, and then home for two or three."

"You think like 200 million other people in this country," I said. "Local drivers tend to get home every night, regional drivers, a couple of days a week, but cross-country or long haul drivers like me are usually out three to six weeks at a time. It's my choice to stay out as long as I do. I once stayed out for over five months."

"Under those circumstances, I can certainly understand how you consider your truck to be your house on the road, but you have to understand that the lab technicians have their job to do."

"So why would they be in my house?"

"I'm not sure but I'd guess they're comparing fingerprints."

"Well they won't find a match," I said.

"And why is that?" Smith asked.

"I was wearing gloves. I always wear work gloves when working around the truck. I've saved myself a lot of minor injuries as a result."

At that point Frank said, "Let's go look at the trailer." The three of us left the car but before we got far, Frank said to Smith, "Agent, I was addressing my client."

Smith stopped and gave Frank a hard stare. For some reason, Smith no longer seemed to be as good-looking as she had earlier. "My orders, Mr. Krandell, were to escort you and your client to the trailer."

"Your orders were to escort us to the yard, and you did, agent. Thank you very much." The two of us turned around and walked to the trailer, leaving Agent Smith by her car.

Although the lab boys were still working, we were able to walk around it after showing our identification. Frank asked me a lot of questions, almost all of them asked before, and I answered them all, again. We went over every place I'd stopped between Slippery Gulch and Reno, but it made no difference, there was still no way I, or anybody else, could have gotten that crusher out of that trailer without removing the seal or cutting away a part of the floor, wall, or top.

We talked to the lab boys and they confirmed the trailer had not been tampered with in any way. Frank asked me if I dropped the trailer anywhere. No. One of the lab boys asked if when I was in the truck, I could feel any movement in the trailer when I wasn't moving. I assured him I could feel as little as a man walking in the trailer, so if you're wondering if a side panel could be removed, the crusher removed, and a side panel replaced without the driver knowing it, even if the driver was asleep, that would be impossible. And I told them, the only time I'm out of the truck for more than an hour is when I stay in a motel. And I didn't stay in a motel on this trip.

Frank said, "Let's head back to the Federal Building and get you on your way."

"Do you think they'll let me go?"

"Oh, they'll let you go," Frank said. "They have no reason to hold you, but is there a way for me to get in touch with you, no matter where you are?"

"Sure, no problem. I have a cell phone in the truck," I said and gave him my number. I also gave him the number of the company. "If you can't get me on the cell phone, call that number anytime of the day or night. Give them my truck number, explain to them who you are, and ask them to have me call you ASAP, unless you have a time in mind. I'll try and return it in a timely fashion but keep in mind that there are times I can't. When in the truck, I can't pull off just anywhere and make a call, and I won't make a call while I'm moving. There are other places in the country where you can go for 70 or 80 miles and never see a pull-off. Some of those roads are right here in your state."

"I know you're right about Nevada," he said.

Once we returned to the car and were in the presence of Agent Smith, none of us said much of anything on our way back to the Federal Building. Once back there, Frank looked up Lurch and asked for the keys to my truck. "Sorry, I can't do that," he said.

"Why?" Frank asked.

"Need I remind you," Lurch said, "that a load was picked up in Montana and was to be delivered to a place in Reno? Although the truck made it, the freight didn't. That's the disappearance of interstate commerce and it just so happens that your client was the driver."

"Everything you just said may or may not be true," Frank said.

"What do you mean by that?" Lurch's eyebrows raised. I looked at Frank as quizzically as Lurch did.

"The missing piece of machinery weighs 2 tons—4,000 pounds, correct?" We both nodded in agreement. "I think both of you would have to agree that nobody could remove 2 tons of equipment quickly and quietly, and yet leave the seal intact. The only way it could be done would be to remove part of the side paneling, inside and out, or remove part of the floor, and then replace everything as it was. Your own lab technicians said no part of the trailer had been tampered with. And furthermore, the Sparks police and the Nevada DOT confirm the original seal was intact."

"So what's your point?" Lurch asked.

"Jake, you saw the crusher being loaded, right?" Frank asked. But before I could answer, he continued, "Or could it be that you only thought you saw it being loaded?"

"Frank, you're losing me," I said. "I was standing right there. I saw him load it." Lurch was silent.

"But did you do anything at all to assist?"

I thought for a minute and said no, but reminded him I secured the crusher after it had been loaded into the trailer.

"Did you have a reason to touch the crusher after it had been loaded?"

After I thought about that for a while, I finally had to say, "No, as best as I could remember." Lurch spoke up, and said, "Where is this going, Krandell?"

"To be perfectly honest, agent, I'm not really sure, but we know two things for certain: The crusher is not in Reno, and the trailer and seal were not tampered with. What that means is that Mr. Winters had nothing to do with the disappearance of the crusher, if in fact it really disappeared at all. Therefore, you have no reason to hold my client."

"Obviously, Krandell, the crusher is missing because it isn't here," Lurch said, "and we know the crusher was loaded onto Mr. Winters' truck. We have a copy of the bill of lading, which your client signed for, and I doubt if he would have signed it if the crusher wasn't on the trailer. We also have a copy of the seal manifest, which Peabody signed. I believe you have a copy of both."

Frank acknowledged that he did and then said, "But if," and cut off his statement. "The point is, agent, you have no reason to detain Mr. Winters any longer. Unless you arrest him for something, he's free to go. You can get in touch with Mr. Winters anytime of the day or night by going through his company, and they can tell you where he is at any time. But let me suggest, since I am legally representing Mr. Winters, that you get in touch with him through me." He handed Lurch one of his cards.

Lurch stood there hesitantly, as Frank said, "Either arrest him now or release him now. It's your choice."

Lurch looked at me, then at Frank, and finally said, "Okay." Handing me the keys and a release form to sign for the tractor he added, "But the trailer stays here, and if I find out you had anything to do with this, I'll have you behind bars so fast, it'll make your head spin."

"That sounds fine to me," I said. I felt like a character in a third-rate film.

"Good. I'll be in touch with you," Frank said to Lurch. With that, we turned around and left the building. Frank gave me a ride back to my truck and on the way, we talked. "You did say your friends from Basin were going into Slippery Gulch yesterday, correct? Let's see. Yesterday was June 30."

"Yeah, they were going in with a sheriff's deputy and a social worker, hopefully to rescue that little boy. They were also going to try and find Peabody. You didn't mention them to the FBI, nor did I. Should we have?"

"No. They will find them soon enough on their own anyway. I'm going to want to talk to them myself. Of course, they have no idea the load is missing."

"Frank, where were you going with the questions you were asking in the federal building?"

"I'm not sure. How much weight can you carry in your trailer?"

"Close to 47,000 pounds."

"So 4,000 pounds isn't very much. Can you even feel 4,000 pounds in the way it handles or pulls? More importantly, if all of a sudden, you were 4,000 pounds lighter, would you feel it?"

"No to both questions."

"So if you thought a 4,000-pound crusher was loaded into your trailer but in reality it was never in there at all, you'd never feel it, correct?"

"That's true, but I know it was loaded. I watched him load it and I secured the damn thing myself."

"It seems to me that the answer somehow lies in the possibility that crusher was never loaded into your trailer. I think somehow what happened and what you think you saw were two different things," Frank said.

"Now wait a minute. There was someone else who saw that crusher loaded into my trailer."

"Oh, who?"

"Peter Stevenson, the little boy. He was there watching me back into the loading zone, and he was there after I closed the doors. I'm sure he was there while Peabody was loading the crusher, but probably hiding, since he was scared to death of Peabody."

"So now it becomes more important than ever to get in touch with your friends in Basin. Let's hope they were able to rescue that boy, for more reasons than one. If there was a witness, it means the load disappeared somewhere between there and here. I want to call your friends right away. Today's Saturday. Would they be there?"

"On a Saturday? I would think so. George was going to be working on his estimated taxes. If he's not there, Jane will be."

"Let's drive out to my office and make the call from there. Nobody's there today, so we'll have all the privacy we need. Do you have the time for this?"

"Are you kidding? If it weren't for you, I could be sitting behind bars right now. I have as much time as you need. I just feel bad about taking you from your fishing on your day off."

"Well, don't. This is building into one of the most fascinating cases I've ever handled. Now if you don't mind, I'd like you to call and explain the situation to this point, including the FBI's involvement. Also, tell them you're calling from my office and ask whoever you're talking to if they would mind if we use the conference phone so we can both hear."

"No problem, but you know, I forgot about the FBI. I hope we can get to them first. I'd rather be the one to explain to them, as best I can, what's going on. Lord knows how the FBI would spin it."

"I don't think that will be a problem," Frank said, as we pulled into a driveway off a four lane road west of town. The building was small but beautiful, sitting on a hill overlooking the city. We got out of the car and walked to the second floor. Inside was a beautiful office with huge windows offering a stellar view of Reno. The walls were all done in Douglas fir paneling, and the desk and chairs were maple. I didn't have long to admire his office or the view. Frank went right to the phone and handed it to me.

While I made the call, Frank made the coffee. After the third ring, Jane picked up the phone. After telling her who I was, there was a long pause and finally she said, "Jake, what's going on?" Now it was my turn to pause but finally I said, "Let me guess. You've heard from the FBI."

"The FBI? No. Why? What's going on?"

Darn, I should have kept my mouth shut, but it was obvious something was bothering her. "Jane, I have a little problem. I'm calling from my attorney's office here in Reno."

"Your attorney? Jake, what kind of a mess have you gotten yourself into? What have you done?"

"Before I attempt to answer that, did you get up to Slippery Gulch? Did you find Peter?"

"Jake, we did get into Slippery Gulch but we've got a lot to talk about. Let me get George. I'll have him get on the other line."

"Would either of you mind if we talk to you on a conference phone? My attorney would like to get involved in this conversation too."

"That's okay with me. Here comes George."

George got on the line and we participated in small talk for a few seconds, then I introduced Frank and explained to them what had transpired since getting to Reno. And why the FBI was involved!

There was a long pause. "Jane and George, you still there?"

George said, "Yeah, Jake, we're still here. Jake, you went into Slippery Gulch to pick up a crusher right? And you did pick it up, didn't you?

"Of course I did. You both know that. Why?"

Jane said, "Jake, we saw the bill of lading, the seal manifest, and even the seal but we didn't see the crusher."

I was really starting to get annoyed. "Of course you didn't, the truck was sealed, but you both knew it was there. Now did you get to Slippery Gulch or not?"

George said, "We did go into Slippery Gulch yesterday, Jake, and we could plainly see by your tracks that you'd been there. But we just don't know how you did it."

At this point Frank cut in before I had a chance. "What do you mean, you don't know how he did it?"

"Well, Mr. Krandell, we did get into Slippery Gulch yesterday as I said. We, meaning Jane, Mike, Beth Jackson the social worker, a deputy sheriff, and myself. Our main purpose for going in was to rescue the little boy and get him out. However, we ran into a little problem. There was a landslide at the cliff, and 20 feet of the road was gone."

"First of all, George and Jane, please call me Frank. Do you think it was the weight of Jake's truck that caused the slide?"

"I didn't go out there with the others," George said, "But Mike called me from the cliff and told me of the slide. At that point, I went out to take a look for myself. Our first reaction was that it happened just as you suggested. But after taking a closer look, we could plainly see that was not the case."

"I don't understand what you're saying, George," I said.

"When we walked out to the damaged area, we found a small, dried streambed with a small amount of weathering and erosion that had taken place. The only thing that could have caused that slide was runoff from the spring snowmelt."

"George, are you saying I never went to Slippery Gulch?"

"No, that's not what I'm saying. We followed your tracks into town. We also followed your tracks up to the mine. There is no doubt you we there; we just don't know how you did it."

"It seems rather obvious, George," Frank said, "that your analysis of the situation is wrong. After all, if you were right, there's no way Jake could have driven across that 20 feet."

"I suppose I could be wrong," George continued, " but I don't think so. There are definite signs of water running right down the middle of the slide and over the cliff. We haven't had any rain in weeks, and the snow pack up in the high country has also been gone for some time. Now you tell me how to explain recent erosion all the way to the cliff, if the road was there the day before."

"I can't," Frank said. "Can you explain to me then how Jake got into Slippery Gulch if the road was already gone by the time he got there?"

"I don't have an answer for you either," George said. "My next question is what happened to the crusher? Jake, are you sure it was loaded into your truck?"

"Of course, I'm sure, I was standing right there. I watched it being loaded. I secured it. In fact, I think Peter saw it being loaded too. By the way, did you find Peter?"

There was another long pause. Finally Frank said, "I think I'm going to have to get up there and talk to both of you and Mike. I'd also like to get in there and see this place for myself. Could someone get me up to the town?"

"No problem," Jane said "As long as you get up there before the snow flies—and it can start flying as early as late August. I think it would be a good idea for you to see everything for yourself."

"I'll be up there within a week. I'll get back to you in a day or two and let you know exactly when. By the way, although we said nothing to the FBI about you folks, I suspect it won't take long for them to show up in Basin, so be prepared."

"What should we say and do?" George asked.

"Answer their questions honestly, but don't volunteer anything."

"Should I mention my suspicions about the erosion?"

"Are you a geologist?" Frank asked.

"Strictly amateur."

"Then don't say a word. And if they ask you to take them up there and they ask you about it, just say you don't know."

"But isn't that withholding evidence or something like that?" Jane asked.

"Right now we have no evidence that a crime truly was committed, so there's no evidence that can be withheld."

That didn't sound quite right to me, but I'm not an attorney, so I kept my mouth shut.

"But the crusher is missing," Jane said.

"True, but the question is, when and where did it disappear?" Frank said. "George or Jane, do either one of you know a geologist in the area?"

"I do," George said. "She's a professor with the University of Montana in Butte."

"Could you contact her and see if you could get her out to the site? Nothing against you, George, but I would like a professional opinion," Frank said. "I would like to be there when she takes a look at it." Frank thought for a moment. "I'll tell you what. I'll set my schedule around her if she's agreeable to come out. I'll give you all of my phone numbers. If you can't get me at one, you'll reach me at another. Call me collect as soon as you talk to her, no matter what she says."

"Okay, but how much should I tell her?" George asked.

"Tell her that you need her professional opinion for an attorney friend of yours who is working on a possible criminal investigation," Frank said. "Tell her also that your friend will be there and can explain it further at that time."

"Okay. I'll try and reach her today and get back to you as soon as possible."

"George, thanks so much for your help and cooperation. I look forward to meeting both of you in the next few days."

Jane said, "We'll do everything we can to help you and Jake, and Jake, drive carefully out there, and we hope to see you again sometime."

"Thanks for everything you're doing. I also hope to see both of you again too. But before you hang up, could you please answer my question?"

There was a long pause, then Jane said, "Jake, we didn't find Peter. We looked everywhere. We even looked in some of the buildings, and we called for him all over town, but found no sign of life anywhere."

"It sounds like they pulled out before you got there," I said. "If so, I don't think that kid stands much of a chance."

George said, "Jake, they couldn't have pulled out early. The road was gone."

I hesitated to say what I did: "I'm sorry, George, but I just don't buy that. I don't care what the geologic evidence shows. I'm the one that drove across that cliff. It was the most hair-raising, nerve-racking experience I've ever had. I watched rocks pop under the weight of my truck and fall over the edge. I was praying, praying my whole truck wouldn't go over the edge next. When I got across, I was dripping wet from sweat even though I had the air-conditioner on full blast. No, George, I'm sorry but I just can't buy that."

"I don't blame you, Jake," George said. "There's nothing about this whole thing that makes any sense at all. Maybe once

I get a geologist up there, she'll provide us with some logical answers."

"I hate to be a cynic, George," Frank said, "but maybe all she'll do is cause us more questions. Nevertheless, I think it's really important we get a geologist up there."

"Yes, I agree," George said. "Hopefully she'll prove me wrong."

"Well, it would sure make it easier if she did," Frank said. "You've got all of my numbers, George. As soon as you find out something, call me collect, day or night."

"Will do," George said. "I'll get on it right away. In the meantime, you be careful out there, Jake."

"Always. George, Jane, good talking to you and I'll call again. Say hello to Mike for me. Thanks for everything."

"You bet. Have a good one, Jake," Jane said and we hung up.

## EIGHTEEN

"Well, what now?" I asked Frank.

"Let's talk for a while. Care for a cup of coffee?"

"Sure, just sugar."

A couple of minutes later Frank came back with the coffee. "So what do you think?" Frank asked.

"I don't think they were telling us everything. I had to ask three times if they found Peter. Each time I asked, they paused a long time as if they were trying to figure out how to answer or change the subject. And when they did answer, all they said was they didn't find him. Why didn't they say that the first time?"

"Yes, I caught that, too." He paused to sip his coffee. "Could it be that since they both knew of your concern, they didn't know how to tell you?"

"That could be part of it, I suppose. But I think they found something pertaining to Peter and either didn't know how to tell me or didn't want to."

"Like what?" Frank shot back.

"I don't know."

"They said they found no signs of him, which means no Peter, no particles of clothing, no tracks, or anything else that pertained to Peter."

"Wait a minute. They had to find some sign of him. I was out of my truck at two different locations in that town talking to Peter. And up at the mine, I was talking to him behind my trailer, so they had to see his tracks by mine. Maybe they meant they found no new signs of him."

"They had to mean that, didn't they?" Frank hesitated. "But they did say they found no sign of him anywhere, right?"

"Yeah, that's what they said, but they had to mean no new signs. Had they seen his tracks from the day before, they could have been taken as new to them."

Frank put in, "Ah, but they would see them in association with yours and not count them as new. Suppose some cult member erased them after you left."

"For what reason? You know, there were times he stepped in my tracks."

"For the sake of discussion, let's assume Peter was never really there."

"Frank, don't get goofy on me. Of course he was there. I saw him, talked to him, touched him, held him, and tickled him! Do you think that can all be attributed to an overactive imagination?"

Frank hesitated and then said, "No, I guess not. They had to be talking about new signs."

Frank sat there deep in thought for several minutes, staring into his cup. Finally I said, "A dollar for your thoughts."

"Well, yes. Indeed." He sat up and drew a deep breath. "They never said a word about Peabody. Curious!"

"Gee, you're right. I never thought to ask. I was fixed on Peter. But they did say they saw no one."

"It's interesting. When I first mentioned Peabody's name to them, everybody said they heard of it, but couldn't remember from where. By the way, speaking of remembering, I have a letter here I was supposed to deliver to Peabody's brother in Reno. He is supposed to own Smith and Associates."

Frank reached over for the envelope. "You mean he used to own Smith and Associates. Remember, it went out of business in 1901."

"Thank you. Where has my mind been? Wait a minute. If it went out of business in 1901, he couldn't be alive. And Peabody shouldn't be as young as he is."

"I know! The more we talk, the less sense we make of the whole thing." He took the letter but didn't open it. I was about to suggest we open it, but I realized I was in the company of a lawyer who knew better.

"The question remains, what happened to the crusher? I've got to get to Basin Monday." With that he took out his pocket calendar, searched through it, and called a number.

"Mary, sorry to call you on a weekend, but something has come up. I'm going to have to fly to Butte, Montana, tomorrow." Mary responded out of my hearing. "Yes, I received it a couple of hours ago. I want you to cancel all my appointments for Monday, Tuesday, and Wednesday. Assign what you can to a paralegal. I should be back Thursday for court appearance. I'll check in with you Monday morning. Thanks a million." Frank hung up and replaced his address book.

"I've got to get you back to your tractor. Then I've got to get home and arrange for a flight to Butte. Oh, I want to call George back and let him know I'm coming in the morning."

"Are you sure you can get a flight out?"

"I have a plane at my disposal. Can you go with me?"

"Oh gee, I wish I could, but I have to get back on the road. But say 'hello' to everyone for me."

"I will. I'll try to call you twice a week, and of course, you can call me anytime." He took a card off his end table and handed it to me.

"Oh, before we leave, may I borrow your phone? I should call my driver manager."

Handing me the receiver, he said, "Sure, be my guest."

I got hold of my DM fairly quickly and explained what I was doing. He said, "I've got a load for you coming to Salt Lake. It's on trailer 002478. The bills are in the office. I'll get all the information out to you right now so when you get to your truck, you'll be all set. Just send me a macro 32 when you're ready to leave. And Jake, when you deliver the load, come right over to the terminal. Some people here want to talk to you."

"I'll get back to you on the computer as soon as I get hooked up," and with that, I hung up.

Frank and I walked out to his car. I told him some people in Salt Lake wanted to talk to me. "How much can I say?"

He stopped in his tracks and thought for a minute. "Maybe it is best to say nothing about the conversation we had with George and Jane. We don't really know what's going on there yet, so limit your remarks to your own experience. And conjecture nothing."

"No problem," I said.

At the impound yard, Frank and I got out of his car, walked up to the security guard, and handed the FBI release form to the guard. Frank and I walked over to the truck. I climbed in and started it. Then the two of us walked around the tractor and trailer. The lab boys were gone. I went back, pulled the release on the fifth wheel, and pulled the tractor out from under the trailer. Then got out and talked to Frank for a few more minutes.

"Well, I'm off to our drop yard for my next load. Do you think the FBI will be in touch with me?"

"I doubt it, but if they are, just tell them to contact me."

"Sounds good to me. Well look, Frank, I really want to thank you for everything you've done so far, and for everything you're going to do. I'd be lost without you."

"I'm not sure if I'd be too quick to thank me for what I haven't done yet. I really don't know what I'm going to do and I don't know where this is going to go. But it's been interesting. I'm certain it's going to become even more so."

We shook hands and I said, "I have faith." I climbed into my truck and headed for the exit, the drop yard, and eventually Salt Lake.

## NINETEEN

I pulled into our drop yard, checked in with security, got my bills for the trip, and started looking for trailer number 002478. I found it without much of a problem, backed under it, hooked the air and electrical lines, and made sure the seal number on the trailer was the same as the number on the bills. Then I brought my logbook up to date. I punched macro 32 into the computer. Macro 32 lets the company computer know what trailer I dropped and where, what trailer I now have, and the seal number on the trailer. This way the company knows where all their trailers are at any given time—or at least that's the way it's supposed to work, and usually it does.

I headed for I-80 and Salt Lake. It was July 1, 3:00 P.M. Pacific time, 6:00 P.M. my time. I wasn't going to get very far tonight. I was tired and frustrated.

I pulled into Sparks, Nevada, earlier that day at about 6:00 A.M. my time, delivering to a consignee that was no longer in existence, and hadn't been for a century. Here I was, my cargo missing and my conduct suspicious. I was the guy with a mysterious disappearing interstate shipment. I was barely out of trouble because of a good attorney fresh out of the Truckee River smelled like fish. Too many more days like this and I would be ready for retirement. Boy, I was beat, and for many good reasons.

In spite of everything, I got a good night's sleep that night and the next. I pulled into Salt Lake City on July 3, in plenty of time for my 7:00 appointment. I emptied out and sent in a macro 14, giving the computer its breakfast. Then I sent a message to my DM to let him know I was on my way back to the terminal. I pulled up to the guard shack and the security guard looked at my truck number and said without a smile, "Oh, you're 9361. The company heavies are waiting for you. Good luck."

This is not the way I'd prefer being greeted by security. As I dropped the trailer, I wondered if this was the last trailer I'd ever drop for this company. All kinds of thoughts were going through my head, none of them pleasant.

As I drove around to the main building, I saw Jason, my DM, standing on the outside landing by the offices waving to me without a smile. The only other time he was waiting for me outside was about a year before when he informed me that my father was on his deathbed and to call home ASAP. His lack of a smile did not look good.

I parked and walked up to him, shook hands as he said, "You know, you're quite a celebrity around here."

"Is that good or bad?" I asked.

"Right now, I don't know. We're going to have a meeting, and you're going to be the guest of honor, so don't go anywhere."

About 15 minutes later I heard my name called over the loudspeaker: "Report to the conference room." I thought to myself, well, here I go. I figured my future with this company could be measured in minutes.

In the room were five men and two women rising from their seats around the table. Jason made the introductions. I knew everyone in the room except one and Jason saved him for last. Included in the meeting were the load planner for Montana, the director of safety in Salt Lake, the director of operations in Salt Lake, the Salt Lake terminal manager, the director of maintenance in Salt Lake, and finally the vice president of operations for the whole company from our home office in Richmond, Virginia. At that point I thought, if they've sent a VP from the main office, I'm dead meat.

Bill Murphy, the vice president, asked us to be seated as he took control of the meeting. He was about my age. He wore wire-rimmed glasses and had steel gray eyes; he looked like a man comfortable with power. He said, "Mr. Winters, you've made quite a name for yourself in Richmond."

This I didn't want to hear. It was getting worse by the minute.

He continued, "I've personally spoken to the Reno police, the Nevada DOT, the FBI, and Mr. Krandell, your attorney. Now we'd like to hear the whole story from your perspective. Why don't you start at the beginning, right from the time you were dispatched on the load in Butte, going right through to the time you left Reno for Salt Lake."

This was going to be a long meeting. I went through my entire story with few interruptions, until I got to the part where Frank and I talked to George and Jane on the phone. I didn't know why I even mentioned it. Mr. Murphy wanted to know the specifics of the conversation. It would have been nice to talk to Frank at that point, but I was on my own.

"There were several strange revelations that came out of that conversation," I said, "enough so that Frank flew up to Butte yesterday to meet with George and Jane personally, and possibly a local geologist. He wanted me to keep that conversation under wraps until he could get some questions answered; so I apologize but I don't think I should get into the specifics until I've talked to Frank."

All were silent for a good 2 minutes, during which time Mr. Murphy rose and walked to a window, as if looking for a new job for me. "Over the years we've had entire rigs stolen, trailers stolen, and freight stolen from trailers; but we have never had freight mysteriously disappear from a trailer with no visible signs of forced entry." He turned to face me. "This is a first. I'm sure there's an answer. I'd be very interested to hear your explanation. I want you to know that until the investigation is complete, the company feels you are the victim of a very unusual circumstance more than anything else. I will continue to be in touch with the FBI and your attorney. If there is anything you'd like to tell me, let me know." And with that, he handed me his card. We shook hands. The meeting was over, and I let out a terrific sigh of relief. I was not going to be fired after all, or at least not yet.

Jason and I stayed behind and talked for a while. He asked, "Was that last part of the trip going into Slippery Gulch as difficult as you indicated?"

"I didn't get into details, but it was by far the most dangerous trip I've ever made. The road was so narrow along the cliff, the outside tires were on the edge. I could see rocks breaking off and falling. I was praying the road would hold. And then after getting loaded, I had to do it all over again."

"My God! When you saw what you were driving into, why didn't you stop and call me?"

"I'd just driven 4 or 5 miles around curves and up and down hills, so backing out was just about impossible. Besides that, I didn't think about calling you. I had a load to pick up and I was anxious to see Slippery Gulch. It sounded neat."

"Was it?"

"Oh yeah, it really was. I'm glad I went in and I'd love to go back someday, just not in a big truck."

He laughed and said, "I think you're crazy."

"Shoot, I've been accused of that before."

He hesitated for a minute and finally said, "Jake, what do you think happened to the crusher?"

"I wish I knew. I know I had nothing to do with its disappearance. And I don't see how it could have been stolen. Why? According to Jane, it may have been an antique but not what you'd call a collectible."

"I wish you'd called me."

"As I mentioned in the meeting, the Nevada DOT can attest to the fact that the original seal was intact and had not been tampered with when I got to Sparks. The FBI lab can attest to the fact that no part of the trailer was tampered with."

"And you watched Peabody load it."

"Yes, I was there the entire time. I was fascinated with the jury-rigged process he used."

"Then you secured the load with wood."

"Correct. Then I got down out of the trailer and closed the doors."

"Did you seal it at that point?"

"No. Peter, the little boy, showed up out of no place and I ended up talking to him for several minutes. Then I grabbed the seal and manifest and walked into the office."

"So at that point, the trailer was left unattended, right?"

"Forget it. I know what you're thinking. While I secured the crusher I saw Peabody remove the harness from his horse and from the tripod, or whatever you want to call it. Then he walked it back to the office. It was then that Peter appeared. I spent some time with him then walked to the office. I wasn't in the office more than 5 minutes. It took Peabody a good 20 minutes to get the crusher into the trailer after he hooked up the horse. Removing it in a short time would be impossible. Not only that, the culprit would have to remove the 2-by-4s first. But they were still there when I got to Sparks. Those were all good questions though. Unfortunately, they don't yield answers. Frank isn't convinced it was ever loaded on the truck in the first place."

"What? He wasn't there!"

"I agree. At one point Frank suggested maybe Peter wasn't really there either. Frank is fumbling over the weird developments since I left there. For instance, George, Jane, Mike, a social worker, and a deputy sheriff went in the next day to rescue Peter. They found there had been a landslide at the killer cliff. About 20 feet of the road was partially gone. It's only about 4 feet wide now."

"So they think the weight of your truck caused the slide?"

"I wish that's what they thought. George said there's evidence the slide happened last winter or early spring. Everything was bone-dry. George is going to have a geologist friend come in and take a look. That's one reason why Frank flew up there. This geologist will know whether George is right or not."

"Now wait a minute, let me see if I understand this. If George is right, the road wasn't there when you drove into Slippery Gulch, correct?"

"That's about the size of it."

"Well, then obviously George is wrong."

"That would be the logical way to look at it. However, they found signs of previously running water, but no sign of immediate water. That's why they're calling in a geologist. If the geologist determines that the slide did in fact take place months ago, this presents a host of other problems since they did find the tracks of my truck going down into Slippery Gulch on the other side of the slide area, and coming back out again."

"Good Godfrey. But if the road wasn't there when you went in, how can you explain that?"

"I can't and I doubt anybody else can. I'm not sure if anybody will ever be able to. I sure didn't carry the truck on my back over the slide area." I thought a moment. "Hey, I really wasn't there."

"Yeah, sure! When you got to the mine, you sent in a macro 3. At that point the satellite pinpointed your location. You also sent me a message saying something about the most difficult trip you'd ever made. You also sent in a macro 32 when you were loaded. All of that is in the computer. We have proof you were there, Jake, so don't freak out on us."

"Of course, the tracks of the truck pretty much prove it anyway."

"That's true. Why didn't you mention any of this in the meeting?"

"Frank didn't want me to mention anything about our conversation on the phone until he had a chance to get up there, look around and talk to the geologist. I'd appreciate it if you'd keep this stuff under lock for now."

"Sure thing. This is certainly going to be fascinating to see how it all plays out. When it's all over, you should write a book about it."

I chuckled and said, "Yeah, right. It's all logical, I guess. But if the geologist determines that the slide happened months before I got there, logic is out the window. Well look, what kind of load do you have for me?"

"I don't know. I'll have to check with the load planners. Hang tight, I'll get back to you."

"Well, you know me, I'd just as soon stay out West for a while."

"No promises, but I'll see what I can do."

I was down in the drivers' lounge drinking coffee and shooting the bull with a couple of other drivers, when my name was called to report to the dispatch. As I walked up, Jason was waiting for me with his usual toothy smile. "I've got a load for you. The miles aren't great, but it's a loaded trailer in the yard going to Nogales, Arizona. It doesn't deliver until the day after tomorrow. It's a drop and hook. You got a 24-hour window. You can drop it anytime between 12:01 and 23:59."

"I've got a couple of friends in Phoenix I haven't seen in a while. This may give me a chance to see them and give my whirling brain a rest. Scenery helps but there's nothing like friends, and an optimistic DM."

"Thanks. Here are the bills. It's trailer 001024. It's a heavy load so scale it before you go too far."

"Yeah, okay. I think I'm going to try and reach Frank. I'll talk to you before I take off."

"You're worried about this, aren't you?"

"Wouldn't you be?"

"I would be and I am. Try and not let it get to you."

"That may be easier said then done. Thanks." I took off for the phones. I tried Frank's cell phone number first and I got lucky. "Frank, Jake Winters."

"Jake, how are you doing? Are you still in Salt Lake?"

"Yeah, heading for southern Arizona. You're still in Montana, I assume?"

"Yes, I'm in Butte. I went up to Basin yesterday and met George, Jane, and Mike. Great people! They took me out to the slide area then into the deserted town. The geologist was not able to meet with us yesterday but we are going to meet her in Basin this afternoon."

"Frank, did you ask them what they meant when the said they found no sign of Peter?"

"For the most part, we guessed right. They meant no new signs."

"What do you mean, for the most part?"

Frank hesitated, "Jake, this is really weird. They found the boy's tracks around your tracks. But when you got in your truck and left, the boy didn't."

"What? What do you mean?"

"You got out of your truck and talked to the boy in three different places: When you first pulled into town, when you were up at the mine behind your trailer, and then when you were leaving town. In all three locations his tracks are plain. But when you left each of those three areas, there were no tracks to indicate he walked away. His tracks indicated he just stayed put. And if that's not enough, according to them, there were no tracks leading up to where he initially met you. It is as though he appeared and disappeared."

"Frank, I paid close attention to those little tracks because of Mike's heads-up back in Basin. I was there. Those tracks did not start mysteriously or end mysteriously. I don't know why but some son-of-a...somebody in that town has erased those tracks."

Frank hesitated again. "Could George, Jane, and Mike have done it?"

I sat there on the phone thinking. I'd only spent two to 3 hours talking to them. How well can you get to know three people in such a short time? But what reason would they have to play games like that? What would be their motive? I was deep in thought when I heard Frank say, "Jake, are you still there?"

"Yeah! Sorry, I was deep in thought. I really don't know them much better than you do. I can't think of any reason why they would erase the tracks. Why would they want to play with my mind like that?"

"I agree, but that's not all."

"Oh great! What else?"

"Remember, they were up there before I ever got there and reported seeing only your tracks and the tracks of the truck. There were no other tracks at all except the boy's tracks over-lapping yours. Tracks of the horse and Peabody were not a part of their report. However, they did find the contraption used to load your truck. But it was in a shambles."

"So there have been either vandals up there or some crazy cult. Either one could explain a lot."

"No, unfortunately, I don't think so. From their description, the contraption used to load the crusher, fell over years ago. The wood was rotten. The metal in the pulleys was frozen in rust. It could not have loaded a bucket of horse manure."

"Impossible! That's just impossible. I saw that machinery working. It was old-fashioned but in working order. They're exaggerating, Frank."

"Well, it certainly sounds like somebody is."

"What do you mean by that?"

"Well, it has occurred to me maybe you could be stretching things. I don't know you all that well, either."

"Look, if you don't believe your own client, maybe it's time I retain a new attorney."

"Don't go off half-cocked. As I said, I haven't been up to the mine yet. Right now I'm just telling you what they told me. I haven't seen it for myself. But once I get up to the mine and see everything is just as they said…Well, put yourself in my shoes. I don't know them or you very well. I would have to conclude at that point one of three things. One, either you're not telling me the whole truth, or two, they're not telling me the whole truth, or three, something else is going on that can't be explained in a conventional way. Do you see my position?"

After I stopped to think about it, I could understand exactly where he was coming from. This whole thing was too strange even for me to believe. I had lived it so how could I expect Frank to believe it. "Yeah, I guess I do. Look, call me when you get back from Slippery Gulch."

"Yeah, I will. By the way, two FBI agents from Butte went up to the slide area with us yesterday and are going in with us this afternoon, if we have time. If not, we'll get in tomorrow. George wasn't very happy about the FBI being here. He's not going to be any happier today, but there's nothing I can do about it."

"Is the FBI still convinced I was responsible for the disappearance of the crusher?"

"Oh, probably! But damn the crusher! They're noncommittal. Don't worry about it though. I'm sure somehow things will work out."

"Easy for you to say. Well, good luck and I wish you well."

"Yeah. Have a good trip and rest well tonight."

"Yep." With that, I hung up. I went back to the dispatch desk to say goodbye to Jason.

"Did you get in touch with your attorney?" he asked.

"Yes. He's going up to the slide area with the geologist this afternoon and then if there's time, they're going into the deserted town and on up to the mine. If not, they'll go in tomorrow. The FBI is with them."

"You sound discouraged, Jake. Do they still think you're responsible for the disappearing crusher?"

" I guess. Nothing I can do about it. I just have to trust Frank. At any rate, I'm not going to take off, as in 'leave the country.' I'll be in touch and, Jason, thanks again for your support."

"Anything I can do, let me know."

"Call the sheriff and see if they have a canine that can sniff out lies, if not missing crushers. That damn thing's going to crush me before this mystery is cracked."

My DM came around the desk and put his hand on my shoulder. I had to fight the waterworks just behind my eyes.

Once I had control of my emotions I said, "You do realize I'm going to have to get back up there sooner or later."

He studied my face and smiled. "You care a great deal for the boy, don't you?"

"He was a neat little kid and I felt sorry for him, but it's not the boy I'm concerned about. It's the crusher and my future."

Never taking his eyes off my face he said, "I understand. In the meantime you have a job to do and so does Frank. He's only been on the job a few days. Give him a chance."

"You're right." Jason's stare unnerved me. Did he see something I did not recognize or understand? "I'll be in touch."

116

## TWENTY

I went out to my truck, fired it up, and drove around to trailer 001024. I needed this run; it was a chance to see some old friends. I was also looking forward to taking a route I hadn't been across for several years: I-15 south to I-70 east; after 30 or 40 miles, then south on U.S. 89. It ran close to both Bryce and Zion Canyons.

From Zion, the Arizona route runs down to Page and across the Glen Canyon Dam that holds back Lake Powell. The lake was named for John Wesley Powell, the first explorer of the Grand Canyon. Thirty-five years ago, Lake Powell was Glen Canyon. Then the dam was built. It is estimated that there were upwards of 6,000 Anasazi sites in the canyon before the lake buried them for all eternity. The lake is about 300 miles long and has thousands of miles of shoreline. Just what a shrink would order.

As I pulled out, I was meditating on the word Anasazi. From what I had gathered, it means "the ancient ones." The Anasazi moved into the area around 950 A.D., built cities in caves and alcoves on the side of cliffs, remained for 200 or 300 years, and then moved on. Nobody seems to know for certain where they came from or where they went. Or why. I was learning that outside my trucking routine, not every why begets an answer.

From Page, U.S. 89 meanders down to Flagstaff. At this time of year, U.S. 89 is packed with tourists. It was a slow go but that gave me time to drink in the scenery. To let it comfort me. I was passed by many cars with kids in them. Often they motioned for me to blow the air horn. When I did, I'd get a much-needed wave and a beautiful smile. A smile from a child can put a smile on a trucker's face just when he needs one. In the middle of some smiles is a large gap where two small teeth are missing, where two larger teeth will come. (Oh, those were the days.) I can't help but think of Peter.

I stayed overnight at a widening in the road called Gray Mountain, about 50 miles north of Flagstaff. Gray Mountain has a warm, homey little restaurant and a gift shop, as well as the usual gas station, convenience store, and motel. There are a few houses there too and that's about all. I ate a steak and called my friend in Phoenix. We agreed where to meet the next day.

I fell into bed and realized why some men have a hard time falling asleep without some sort of companionship on certain trying nights.

The next morning on July 3, from Flagstaff, I took I-17 south to Phoenix. I-17 can be a treacherous route: There are several 6 percent downgrades and a number of elk cross the highway. This beautiful challenge kept me alert and served me well.

Once I got to Phoenix, I parked the truck in a shopping plaza and walked to the little restaurant we'd earlier agreed on. I was a little early but didn't have long to wait. After about 5 minutes I looked out to see a very attractive young women bounding across the parking lot with the energy I wish I still had. Kathy Pawlanski was the daughter of a very good friend of mine back home. Mary was the camp nurse in a camp I'd worked at 20 years ago. She decided to bring her 9-year-old daughter to camp with her and the rest is history. She was living in Phoenix and finishing her doctorate in pharmacology. Not only is she good-looking and intelligent but she has an abundance of common sense.

We greeted each other with a big hug and kiss. We sat down to talk. She filled me in on the pitfalls of going for a doctorate, something I'd never have to worry about. (I've always had a great deal of respect for anybody who was willing to put in the sacrifice of time, energy, and money.) She was just starting to fill me in on some of our mutual friends when she looked outside and squealed, "Oh, here comes Rob."

I looked out the window to see a young man holding the hand of a small boy, walking him across the parking lot. It was Rob and his son, Jimmy. (Lord, where does the time go?) It seemed like just yesterday: Nineteen years ago Rob walked into my cabin as a boy himself. Seven or eight at the time, he had wavy, dark hair and engaging blue-gray eyes. The 4-year-old's hand he now held had Rob's same hair. As they came close I saw the same blue-gray eyes—he was the spitting image of his father. Kathy and Rob met at that camp, when I was assistant camp director. Both went all the way through the program and eventually became staff members themselves. What good friends. Both ended up in Phoenix at about the same time. (No, Kathy is not the mother of Jimmy, just Jimmy's non-blood aunt.) Jimmy's mother was working at the time and couldn't make it.

Since I hadn't seen Jimmy since he was a year old, I didn't recognize him. He certainly didn't recognize me.

The three of us talked for about 2 hours. I sketched for them my latest adventures in Montana; Jimmy was bored much of the time. Once in a while I'd entertain him with a story about his dad when Rob was a little guy. Jimmy loved those.

Finally came the time to go. All four of us went out to my truck and Rob and Jimmy climbed in and looked around. They both thought it was pretty neat and then the three of us climbed out.

We all said our final goodbyes. I gave Kathy another big hug and kiss and shook Rob and Jimmy's hands. I climbed back into the truck and started it with a mighty roar. Jimmy motioned to me, and I blew the air horn. He covered his ears but gave me a beautiful smile, the same smile I'd seen before 19 years ago. And then I left. When would I see them again? Lord only knows.

I drove east on I-10 to Tucson where I stayed for the night. I'd picked up I-19 going south to Nogales the next morning. Nogales is a border town and like all border towns with Mexico, it's a tough place. It's the type of place where you take care of business and get out before it gets dark. If not, you lock your doors and don't leave your truck. You say your prayers and hope for the best. Then you're glad to see daylight!

When I got down there the next morning, I found I had lucked out. Although it was July 4 and everything was closed, the security guard was there and could take care of all my paperwork. After dropping my trailer and getting the papers signed, I had a loaded trailer waiting for me going to Lincoln, Nebraska. I was to be out of there in 15 minutes, and that's just the way I liked it.

From there I headed north on I-19, again back to Tucson, and then east on I-10 to Las Cruces, New Mexico; then north on I-25 to Denver, where I'd pick up I-76 east to I-80 and ran that to Lincoln. I-25 is an energizing desert route running through Albuquerque, then north through Santa Fe up to Raton and through Raton Pass into Colorado. The original Santa Fe Trail ran through Raton Pass in the early 1800s from St. Louis to Southern California.

I didn't have to be in Lincoln until the afternoon of the July 6, so I had plenty of time. I decided to go as far as Albuquerque and stay at The Flying J truck stop, another large high-quality nationwide chain. It would be a nice change to get into the high country. It was supposed to be 118 degrees in Tucson that day. It might only be 95 or so in Albuquerque.

The next morning, I got up and grabbed a cup of coffee, hitting the road by 6:00 Eastern time. Although it was early in New Mexico, there was already a little light in the eastern sky. The mountains west of I-25 would be magnificent as the sun rose. I decided to drive to Springer, New Mexico, for breakfast. It's about 200 miles or 3½ hours north of Albuquerque.

At about 9:30, I pulled into the lot of a relatively small truck stop in Springer and noticed another QZX truck parked there. This wasn't the least bit unusual, there are so many company drivers. I really didn't pay any attention to it since I know very few of the drivers. I walked into the restaurant with an eye on a vacant table in the back. I was paying attention to nothing except my own thoughts when I heard someone say, "Hey, you old coot! What are you doing here?"

I looked toward the voice and without cracking a smile said, "Oh man, I've been going out of my way for the past year to avoid you. I must have taken a wrong turn."

"Well, I'm not excited about seeing you either. But since we're both here, what should we do about it?"

"I suppose we could have a cup of coffee together."

"I could handle that, if I must." Henry "Hank" Hamilton stood up and we shook hands. Hank was a driver I'd known for close to 10 years. A very good friend, we always take friendly jabs at each other even though we go 1 or 2 years between visits. "Have a seat," he said.

"I would, but I really don't like to be seen with senior citizens." Hank was just about a year older, and I always reminded him of it. We sat down, both trying to keep straight faces.

I said, "Where are you headed?"

"Omaha."

"You're kidding. I'm going to Lincoln. Hey, if you don't mind running with a mere youngster, we could run as far as Lincoln together."

Feigning deep thought, he said, "I guess I can handle it."

We then brought each other up to date on where we'd been and what we'd been up to since we'd last met—1 year before at a truck stop in Barstow, California.

Hank and I first met in one of the most unlikely places in the United States. I was on my way to Snowflake, Arizona, from Phoenix to pick up a load. I had to cut up U.S. 60 through Salt River Canyon. The road going down into the canyon was a 9 to 10 percent grade with hairpin turns. If you lost your brakes, you had two choices. You could go over the cliff on the right and kiss it goodbye or you could bounce off the cliff on the left before sending you over the cliff on the right and then kiss it goodbye.

When I reached the bottom, there was a small rest area with truck parking for two. And there sat another company truck. So I stopped to see who the other driver was and where he was going. I stepped up to the one remaining urinal and said, "You know, we've got to stop meeting this way." It was Hank, and he was loading at the same place I was. That day began our incidental meetings.

Hank is about 5-foot-10 and average size. He has less hair than me. He always wears a Detroit Lions baseball cap so it's hard to see how much or how little is left. After loading in Snowflake that day, we decided to run together since he was going to Illinois and I was going on to Indiana. Our plans got jerked around. He was on Pacific time and I was on Eastern. So at 9:00 my time, I was ready for bed; it was only 6:00 his time, and he wanted to run for another 3 or 4 hours.

In the morning I'd be on the road by 5:00 and it would only be 2:00 his time. So about 8:00 my time we stopped for dinner and parted ways not knowing if or when we'd ever see each other again. The two of us had hit it off at once, and we've been the best of friends ever since. Now that Hank lived in the Eastern time zone, where I did, time was not against us running together. It was so refreshing to run with somebody you could just shoot the breeze with and forget what was bothering you for an hour or so. But finally you want to let your friend in on your life.

After agreeing to run together I said, "Hank, I know you've had a lot of interesting experiences out on the road, probably more than me. Of course, you're older so that should be expected. No matter what experiences you've had in the past though, I think I now have you beat." I sketched my latest experience in Slippery Gulch with the phantom crusher. Although I did not get into all the details, I explained in detail the driving back and forth across the cliff and the drive up to the mine and back down again.

As a driver, he could relate to everything I was saying. When I had finished explaining the driving part he said, "You don't really expect me to believe that, do you?"

"To be perfectly honest, not really, but it's true. But listen to this." I told him a little about Peter and Peabody and about the folks in Basin, but when I got to the missing crusher in Reno, that was just too much.

"Wait a minute. That's impossible. There's no way you can get into a trailer without destroying the seal or part of the trailer. You come up with this tale on your own, or did you have help?"

"Hank, this isn't a story. I haven't exaggerated any part of it. The FBI is not the least bit amused and I am now under suspicion somehow of being involved in the disappearance of interstate freight."

"You're kidding? The FBI is involved?"

"It involves interstate commerce, Hank. And before you ask, yes, I have an attorney."

"You're really serious about this, aren't you?"

"Oh, I couldn't be more serious. And the worst part is, I really don't know where this is going to land me. I'm having to put my confidence in my attorney."

"How did you find an attorney in Reno on a Saturday?"

I explained that whole process of finding Frank and my talk with the FBI, and he was amazed. "Under that kind of pressure, how could you think so clearly?"

"You remembered Ruby Ridge and Waco?"

"Yeah."

"If it weren't for Frank, I'd more than likely be in jail in Reno right now. They wanted to hold me right then, but Frank got me released. Before we leave, I'm going to call Frank and see where we stand and what he's found out."

Hank had a lot of questions, most of which I couldn't answer. The subject finally shifted to other things, such as where we'd been in the last year, and what we'd seen and done. Finally it was time to call Frank. Hank asked if I wanted him to leave. I appreciated his respect for my privacy, but I didn't feel it was necessary.

I got through to his secretary on the second ring. I was on hold for just a few seconds when Frank came on. "Jake, how are you doing and where are you?"

"I'm doing fine and I'm in Springer, New Mexico. I'm on my way to Lincoln, Nebraska. What's going on? Did you meet with the geologist? What did—?"

He cut in. "What a minute. Let's take it one question at a time. In fact, how about if I tell you what happened and what I've learned and then it will be your turn for questions."

"Okay," I said reluctantly, knowing it was best to keep quiet and listen. I noticed when I mentioned "geologist" Hank looked up. That was part of the story I hadn't told him.

"We had planned to meet with the geologist Sunday afternoon in Basin and go up to Slippery Gulch. But her 10-year-old daughter fell out of a tree and broke her arm. We had to postpone everything until the next morning."

"We all met at the Silver Saddle Saloon at 9:00 A.M. I can sure see why you think so much of George, Jane, and Mike. They are fine folks. They had coffee and donuts ready for all of us, and Jane fixed enough food to feed a trucker. We took it with us up to Slippery Gulch."

"Who do you mean when you say 'we all'?"

"It was quite a party really. There were George, Mike, and Jane, the geologist, two FBI agents, the local sheriff, and myself. It would have been nice had the geologist and me been alone. But I couldn't keep the FBI away. Or for that matter the sheriff either."

"No, I suppose not."

"The geologist—her name is Renee Armsburger—confirmed the fact that the slide happened earlier, probably in April during the spring melt."

"Frank, that's impossible." Hank looked up again. "If the slide happened in April, how did I drive across it in June?" Hank was giving me a quizzical look.

"None of us have an answer to that."

"How competent do you think this Renee Armsburger is?"

"Well, I'm not a geologist and my knowledge is rather lacking in the subject, but George has apparently always been quite interested in geology. He has a couple of college classes under his belt. Renee was his professor. She's a Ph.D.—a full professor. She's quite qualified. But, Jake, even with my lack of knowledge in the subject, I could see that we're not talking a recent slide."

"This is screwy."

"Yes, I agree. Look, I hired George to do some digging into the history of Slippery Gulch and J and J mines."

"Why?"

He hesitated for a minute. "It can't hurt."

"Do you know something I don't know? Did any of you go into Slippery Gulch?"

"Yes, we all went in but they say nothing had changed. There were no new tracks. The place seemed to be completely deserted and appeared to have been for a very long time. I did see the boy's tracks just as George and Jane explained. And of course, after Renee examined the slide area and determined it did happen earlier in the year. Everyone was dumbfounded as to how your tire tracks could continue on the other side. No one could come up with a reasonable explanation. I believe the FBI is convinced there's some kind of trickery going on. Look, is there any possibility you could stay in the West for a while?"

"I can try."

"I have a feeling the FBI is going to want you up here before too long. And to be perfectly honest, I think it would be fitting."

"Do you think I'm going to get nailed with this?"

"Don't lose any sleep over it."

"Now you sound like a politician."

He let out with what sounded like an uncomfortable chuckle and said, "No, I don't think so."

"I hope you're right. Look, as far as staying out West goes, would you mind calling my DM and requesting that?"

"That's fine." He read off the number that I'd given him earlier, just to confirm it.

"Keep me posted."

"Will do. And God's speed, Jake."

"Always."

# TWENTY-ONE

Hank looked at me and said, "Well?"

"Well what?"

"Well, are you going to prison?"

"I hope not but this whole thing is really getting interesting. I didn't tell you everything. I told you about driving along the cliff. Well, there's been a landslide that took out a portion of the road."

"You're kidding. Was it the weight of your truck that caused it?"

"That would be the most logical assumption. That's what I thought when I first heard about it. But it seems logic doesn't count in this case. A geologist looked at it and determined it happened during the spring melt, probably sometime in April."

"Then it was reopened?"

"That's the problem. No!"

"If the slide happened in April and it was not repaired, how could you get through in June?"

"That's the million-dollar question. When they walked across the slide area, my tracks were as clear as a bell continuing into town."

"That's impossible. If the road no longer exists, you couldn't have gone on."

"That seems rather obvious, doesn't it? Yet when I went through, the road was there. But all evidence says it wasn't."

"That doesn't make sense."

"Tell me about it. But that's not all." I told him that there was no sign of Peabody, the horse, or Peter, including tracks. I also told him about the ruined machine.

126

This last bit of information was just too much. "None of this makes any sense. If the machinery was rusting and rotten a few days ago, it would have been in the same shape when you were there unless you weren't really there. Jake, I consider you one of my best friends, but you've put me in a position where I have to say, I can't believe this."

"Would it help to see the bill of lading and seal manifest?"

"Yeah, it would."

"That's my only proof I was there. Well, that and the pictures."

"What pictures?"

"I took several pictures of Peter, a picture of the town from the hill as I was leaving and a couple pictures of the road going across the cliff."

"You're kidding? How did they turn out?"

"I don't know. I haven't gotten them developed yet."

"Why not?"

"I haven't finished the film yet."

"Who cares, you dummy! That's your proof you were there. Did you take pictures of Peabody and the machinery? How about the crusher sitting in your truck?"

"No, I didn't. They would have been great pictures but I didn't think of it until I was leaving and ran into Peter. Then I thought about Peabody and the mine but I wasn't about to go up there again."

"Does your attorney know about the pictures?"

"I don't know. I can't remember if I told him or not."

"Why doesn't that surprise me. Let's stop someplace and get them developed."

"Okay. I am a little curious as to how they turned out but I hate to develop a role when I haven't finished it. Let's go out to the truck and I'll show you the bills and the seal manifest."

As we walked out to the truck Hank said, "You know, I can't believe how cheap you are. You've got pictures proving you were there and you don't get them developed because you're not finished with the roll. Sorry, Jake, but under the circumstances, that's stupid."

"Yeah, I guess you're right." Upon reaching my truck, I grabbed the bills and seal manifest. He took one look at the bills and said, "What is this?"

I starting laughing and said, "I told you there wasn't any electricity in the town or machinery and that includes a typewriter."

He looked at the seal manifest and Peabody's signature. "You're really serious about this, aren't you?"

"That's what I've been telling you. Come on, let's get moving." Hank walked over to his truck. We were soon headed for I-25 and southern Colorado.

We pulled into a Wal-Mart in a small town and walked in, my film in hand. In 1 hour I would have my proof. We spent the hour eating lunch in a fast-food joint next door. Finally it was time. We walked to the photographic department; I paid for the pictures, and then out to Hank's truck to look at them. The first few were scenery pictures somewhere in the West and then finally the first picture of Slippery Gulch and Peter. There stood a very sad little boy but something was wrong. Although the town in the background was perfectly clear, Peter was somewhat transparent. I handed the picture to Hank as I looked at the next one. Peter had a slight smile on his face, but in the third, Peter was obviously laughing. It was a much better picture, but Peter was still somewhat transparent. The fourth picture, taken from the top of the hill, apparently was taken from too far away. The little boy was nowhere to be found.

"How could they mess up these pictures like this?"

"I don't think they did. They look like double exposures to me," Hank said. "I think you forgot to advance your film."

"Yeah, they do. The only problem is, I can't take double exposures with my camera without making a couple of adjustments and I didn't make any."

"How old is your camera?"

"About 15 years."

"Then your camera is like you, it's no spring chicken. Couldn't it have malfunctioned?"

"I suppose that's a possibility. In fact, in looking at these pictures, that's probably the only possibility. I think I'm going to run them back inside and see what they say."

At the photography department, I pulled the pictures in question out and pointed out the problem to a technician. "What's your best guess as to what happened here?" I asked.

"The only thing that could cause that is a double exposure," she said. "What kind of camera are you using?"

"A 15-year-old Olympus."

"More than likely that's your answer. Even though you aren't supposed to be able to take a double exposure with that camera, it's old and probably malfunctioned."

"I suppose you're right. Thanks for your time."

On the way back to the trucks, Hank said, "Wait a minute. Didn't you say you took a couple pictures of the road going across the cliff?"

"Oh, yeah. I forgot about them." I went through the pictures again. I took one look at them and said, "Oh my God, I don't believe it."

I handed him the two pictures. "Is this the cliff?"

"Yeah. That's it all right."

Continuing to look at them, he said slowly, "That road doesn't look wide enough for a truck."

"That road isn't. Half of it's gone. But it can't be. I walked across it and took this picture looking at my truck. I then drove across it."

"I have no idea what's going on but don't you think you should tell your attorney about the pictures?" Hank asked.

"I guess I should if I haven't already. Let's get going." We headed for Denver where we stayed the night. After a good dinner, I called Frank.

It was 6:00 our time; only 3:00 Frank's time. Again I got through quickly. After talking to his secretary for a minute Frank came on the line. "Sorry to bother you again but I thought you'd be interested in this. I got my pictures developed."

"Don't worry about it. What pictures?"

"Shoot, I guess I forget to tell you. I took three pictures of Peter and two pictures of the road going across the cliff." Hank gave me a knowing look. "I took the pictures of Peter before I left Slippery Gulch. I took another from the top of the hill overlooking the town."

"How'd they come out?"

I explained the results and how I thought my camera malfunctioned producing the double exposures but I couldn't explain the road. There was a pause then, "Did you get a picture of Peabody, the mine, or the machinery?"

"No. I didn't think of it until I ran into Peter as I was leaving town. At that point, I wasn't about to go back up to the mine."

"I guess I can't blame you. You said when you took the picture of the town from the hill, Peter was standing in the center of town, but when you saw the picture, Peter wasn't there? How do you explain that?"

"I guess I was too far away, or he was too small."

"I suppose. I talked to your driver manager. Once you unload in Lincoln, they're going to send you back to Salt Lake. Then we'll go from there. Okay?"

"Sounds good. I'll try and not bug you for a while."

Meanwhile Hank was waving his hand trying to get my attention. He handed me his napkin with the word cliff on it. "Frank, I almost forgot," Hank was shaking his head. "I took two other pictures on the way out, both of the cliff."

"Oh? How did they turn out?"

"For the most part, fine. The coloring is perfect and they're both crystal clear."

"But?" Frank seemed to know what was coming.

"But," I hesitated, "half the road is gone."

"Did you take the pictures before or after you drove across it?"

"That's the problem. I took them before. Frank, this is impossible."

Frank said slowly, "I know." He hesitated. "Jake, there's an answer out there to everything that's going on and we're going to find it. It's just that I'm not sure we're going to understand it."

"What do you mean by that?"

He didn't answer me. "Anytime you come up with anything at all, call me. I'm anxious to see those pictures. By any chance, when you got them developed, did you get two copies of each?"

"Yeah, I did."

"Terrific. I'm really looking forward to seeing them. The FBI doesn't know about them, do they?"

"No. If I forgot to tell you then I'm sure I never said anything to them."

"Good. I think we'll just keep it that way until it becomes necessary. Well look, I'd better get going. I'll be in touch—and, be safe out there."

"Always." I played with the napkin. "Frank, thanks again for everything."

"You bet."

Hank looked at me. "So, you old fart, you forgot to tell him."

"Yeah, I did but the good thing is, I didn't say anything to the FBI either." I continued fiddling with the napkin.

"Well, I guess that's good," Hank said with uncertainty. We sat quietly for a few minutes. He looked at the pictures again. "Good-looking kid." He paused. "You're worried about him, aren't you?"

"Peter doesn't mean anything to me," I answered harshly. "I'm worried about the crusher and my future. I could care less about the kid."

"You're a liar." I looked at him, angry about being challenged. "Sorry for being so blunt but we've known each other a long time. Even though we don't see one another that much, we know each other well. I can see it in your eyes, Jake. Sure you're worried about the crusher and your future but you're worried about that kid too. If you weren't, you wouldn't be human."

I played with the napkin some more. I finally looked at him and nervously laughed. "You're right, Hank. I am worried about him. I just wasn't willing to admit it until now, not even to myself." I looked at the napkin I'd torn to shreds. "I hope he's okay, wherever he is."

"I knew you were human." We both laughed then sat around shooting the bull for a couple of hours. It really helped. On the way out to our trucks I thanked him for being my friend, even if he was old.

## TWENTY-TWO

The next morning we had our coffee to go and were on the road by 5:30. We turned the CB radios to channel 15, and except for breakfast and our Rush Limbaugh break from noon to three, we shot the bull for 500 miles. We had dinner in Lincoln before separating. Hank would drive on to Omaha for his morning delivery. Before taking off, he said, "Look, you've got to stay in touch and let me know how this darn thing turns out. Okay, my friend?"

I promised I would. Anytime either one of us would get to a terminal, we'd send a message to the other, via the computer, to call the other at that particular terminal. It was easy. We'd been using this system for years, but not on a regular basis. We both threw out a few fun-loving insults, shook hands, and reminded each to be careful out there. Hank took off without either of us knowing when we'd run into each other again. At least we'd keep in regular contact.

The next morning, after unloading, I repowered a load going straight to Salt Lake City. An example of a repower would be a driver picking up a load in Point A and going to Point C. For whatever reason when the driver can't deliver it to Point C, he or she drops the trailer in Point B. In this case, Point B was Lincoln, Nebraska. Another driver then comes into Point B, picks up the trailer, and delivers the load to Point C. I was the other driver and Point C was Salt Lake City.

The trip out was uneventful until I stopped at Cabela's, a terrific store for outdoor enthusiasts in Sydney, Nebraska. I should never stop there. I never get out without spending my hard-earned money on something I think I need.

The trip along I-80 through Wyoming was as beautiful as ever. In the eastern part of the state and to the south, the Colorado Rocks are visible on and off for 150 miles. For the last 100 miles in the west are the Uintas; the highest mountain range in Utah. Between east and west are many other smaller mountains and a lot of wide-open space. It was just past the scales at Evanston, Wyoming, where I picked up my tail, which turned out to be the FBI.

After saying goodbye to Jason, I grabbed the stuff I needed for a week and left with the agents for the airport. On the way I said, "Does my attorney know about this?"

"Of course he does. In fact he's up in Butte waiting for us right now," McCade said. It was July 7, less than a week after my load had disappeared. I was on my way to Slippery Gulch again.

I tried to get Frank on the cell phone but failed. So I tried his office in Reno. His secretary gave me his motel number in Butte, but again there was no answer. I left a message for him to call me. I called his beeper and then hung up and waited for his return call. It never came.

We reached the airport and drove right out to a small, private jet marked United States of America on it. McCade and I boarded it while Jones took the car and drove off. The flight to Butte was quick and awesome. But I was unable to enjoy it, distracted by my nebulous status. Where would I be in 24 hours? Would I be a free man or sitting in jail somewhere?

After leaving the plane, the first two people I saw were Lurch and Smith. Then Frank walked out of the terminal. Was I glad to see him! At the same time, I was madder than hell. I ignored Lurch and Smith, walked up to Frank, and said, "Frank, what in heaven's name is going on? Why didn't you let me know about all of this?"

"Jake, I don't blame you for being upset. The FBI and I both wanted you up here. I've been tied up with George. He's come up with a lot of very interesting information from the Jefferson County Historical Society. I think we finally have some answers."

"Oh, I'm interested," I said with a hint of sarcasm.

"I don't think you're going to like it. And the FBI is not accepting our theories. Their agents from Reno have not been to Slippery Gulch yet but once they are, hopefully, with your help, we'll have the whole picture. Let's get you into a motel and grab a bite to eat. Then we're going to Basin and meet with George, Jane, and Mike."

"Did they find Peter?"

"Well, yes and no."

"What do you mean by that?"

"I'm going to let George explain."

"Frank, cut the smoke screen!"

"Let's just say that when you were in Slippery Gulch, nothing was as it appeared."

"How so?"

"Did you bring your pictures with you?"

"I did."

"When we get to your motel room, I want to take a look at them."

The four of us drove to the motel. Lurch and Agent Smith asked questions I'd already answered. Did they think I lied? Or forgot?

After settling into the motel, I went over to Frank's room with the pictures. There was the one of a very sad, little boy. The next was of Peter with a slight smile. The third was with a big beautiful smile. Frank studied the three of them for a minute and said, "So this is the infamous Peter. Cute kid, but sadder than hell, and terrified. How did you get him to smile in this one?"

"Before taking the first one I told him to smile but as you can see he didn't. So before taking the second, I put the camera down, grabbed him, and tickled him in his ribs. By the time I got back to the camera, the smile had just about faded. So before taking the third, I told him if he didn't smile, I was going to tickle the living daylights out of him. I got him laughing."

"You actually physically tickled him?"

"How else can you tickle someone if you don't do it physically?"

"Of course, you're right! I just don't understand how...I don't see...look, these pictures are not double exposures, are they?"

"No, I don't think so, but I don't understand what happened."

"And in this picture," Frank said holding up the fourth, "you could see Peter standing in the street through the lens when you took the picture?"

"Yeah, I could."

"Do you have any theories as to why he's not in the picture?"

"No, but I've got a feeling you do."

He ignored my statement and went to picture number four, the first picture of the missing road across the cliff. "You took this picture then drove across the road, you said?" He didn't wait for an answer. "You were on your way out, right?"

"Right, but how could I if it really wasn't there? Take a look at the last picture. In this one, you see the narrow road where I'm standing next to my truck. No doubt the missing road was between my destination and where I stood. But you do have an explanation for the pictures of Peter, don't you?"

"I didn't say that. Look, it's time to go." And with that I was dismissed, so to speak. Through lunch (or breakfast, depending what time zone people were in), not much of importance was discussed. I didn't eat much. I was anxious to get to Basin and see my friends again and maybe to finally find out what was going on. Frank knew a lot more than what he was saying, and he was driving me crazy.

After what seemed like hours, we were finally on our way to Basin. The trip up was as beautiful as before. The only difference was that I wasn't driving. Soon we pulled up in front of the Silver Dollar Saloon. Before we could get to the door, it opened and out walked George, Jane, and Mike, and another woman I did not know but who I was looking forward to meeting. She was in his early thirties, dark complexion, long, dark brown hair, and the most beautiful hazel eyes I'd ever seen. Jane said her name was Tasha Milinski. Jane did not say who this lady was or why she was here. And I didn't ask, yet. Lurch and Smith seemed to be as perplexed as I was but Frank had obviously met her before.

All had smiles on their faces, but I sensed something was different. I shook hands with George and Mike and gave Jane a big hug. We went inside and shot the bull for a while over coffee. When it was time to get down to business, I put in, "George, Frank told me you found Peter."

"That's not exactly what I said, Jake," said Frank. "When you asked me I said yes and no."

"Yeah, okay, you're right, Frank. Now what does he mean by that, George?" George looked down at the table. I looked at Mike. He started stirring his coffee. I looked at Jane, but she got up to get another cup. Tasha looked at Frank. Lurch and Smith sat there looking as confused as I was. Not one of them said a word. Finally I said, "Look, apparently everybody in here knows what's going on except me, and I'm the one most involved."

Finally, Frank said, "Jake, show everybody those pictures you took."

"What pictures?" Lurch asked.

Frank ignored the question and said, "Why don't you start with the three you took of Peter first." I noticed the two FBI agents give Frank a really strange look, but I pretended not to notice. I started passing the pictures around in the order I'd taken them. When they got to Tasha, she spent time studying each one. Was she a professional photographer? Jane got them last. At the sight of the three pictures of Peter, she started crying. Mike got up and walked over to her. I said softly, "Jane, what's wrong?"

"Oh, Jake, I'm so sorry." She breathed. Mike gave her a hug. "Jane, what's wrong? What's going on?"

"Jake—" she choked on her words. "Jake, Peter's dead."

I sat there stunned. Did I hear her right? Jane continued: "There was nothing any of us could have done, Jake. Peter was right when he told you his father would kill him, but how could you know; all children say that at one time or another. As best we can figure, somehow his father found out that Peter told the driver about his father's threat to Peabody. He caught Peter in the street the next day, beat him to the ground, then stabbed him repeatedly and fled. By the time people got to him, he was dead from multiple stab wounds to the stomach and chest. His father has not been seen since."

"Wait a minute. You were there in town the next day."

"Let me take it from here, Jane," George said. "Jake, we were there the day after you were, but not the day Peter was murdered."

"Now you've lost me."

"Yeah, I thought I would," George said. "According to the history of the town, you were not the first driver to pick up that crusher. And the last time it was picked up, it disappeared then, too. However, the first driver was in there exactly 100 years ago to the day that you showed up."

"George, I'm sorry but you're not making any sense. A crusher could have been picked up 100 years ago, but obviously it was another one." Lurch and Smith were strangely quiet.

George continued. "In 1885 two prospecting brothers by the name of Jacob and Jeremiah Peabody moved into the area. They were prospecting for gold but discovered copper instead—a lot of it, or so they thought. They started up a mine, hired a number of men to work it, and founded the town of Slippery Gulch.

"About 5 years later, the two brothers apparently had a falling out, so Jacob decided to strike out on his own. Jeremiah bought out Jacob and Jacob left for California, stopping in Reno for a while.

"There he was offered a job and began moving up in a company quickly. The company was Smith and Associates. By the way, this part of the story was picked up by one of Frank's associates in Reno."

I sat there totally and completely mesmerized, hardly believing any of this. George continued. "Jacob eventually became executive vice president of the company. A short time later, the owner of the company, a man by the name of Smith, was killed as a result of a fall from a horse, in an apparent accident. Jacob took over the company and kept the Smith name."

"Jacob had connections with some miners in the area, and when he heard that Jeremiah was closing the mine, he had an immediate buyer for the crusher, a small mine over near Virginia City. He contacted his brother and made arrangements to have the crusher shipped. Before the crusher could make it to Reno, Jacob was killed in a barroom brawl. Six months later his company went belly-up. So you see, the theft of the crusher was all for naught; but of course, whoever was responsible for it didn't know that."

"Meanwhile, back in Slippery Gulch, Peabody made many enemies. One of them was Peter's father."

Suddenly everything hit. "Wait a minute. Are you trying to tell me Peter died 100 years ago, that he's a ghost?" I stood up and walked to the bar. "No, I can't buy that crap. Peter is not, and was not a ghost. I held him, tickled him. I took pictures of him. You can't do any of those things with a ghost."

Tasha suddenly cried, "That's impossible!"

I gave this unknown woman a hard stare. "Look, lady, I don't know who you are, I don't know what you are, and I don't even know what you're doing here, but don't try and tell me what's impossible."

Jane got up and came over to me. "Peter was right," I said. "I should never have told Peabody. I should never have left that town without him. He asked if he could go with me, but I said no."

I had been blaming myself for his death. I was struggling to control my emotions and guilt but I guess Jane missed that.

Jane said, "Jake, don't take it out on Tasha. It's my fault you and the rest of you don't know who Tasha is. I just wasn't ready yet to properly explain her presence. I didn't think the rest of you were ready either. First of all, Tasha is a very good friend of mine and second, Tasha is a very good and reputable parapsychologist."

"Oh for cripe's sake, a ghostbuster," Smith bellowed. "This has nothing to do with ghosts but everything to do with missing freight."

"I disagree, agent," Frank said. "I think this has everything to do with ghosts. I hired George to dig into the history of Slippery Gulch. What he came up with leads me to believe the crusher was never shipped 100 years ago and is still in the vicinity of the mine somewhere."

"That's ridiculous," Smith said. "Winters saw the crusher being loaded into his truck."

"What he saw, I believe, was an apparition. In fact, I believe everything Jake saw in Slippery Gulch was an apparition, which is why I asked Jane to invite Tasha here today."

"But the pictures. I've never seen a picture of an apparition before. Peter can't be a ghost," I insisted.

Jane walked over to the table. "Jake, look at these pictures. They look like double exposures, but I'm willing to bet they're not. And this picture looking back into town! Didn't you say Peter was standing in the street?"

"Yes."

"Well, where is he in the picture? Were you too far away to get a picture of him? I don't think so. Jake, you have to accept the fact that Peter is dead and has been for 100 years. There isn't a thing you could have done to change that fact. You got there 100 years too late. That's why Frank thought a parapsychologist could be helpful." She looked at Frank then both looked at Tasha and so did I.

Tasha glanced at the others and fastened her gaze on me. "Jake," she said slowly, "I apologize for coming on so strongly. I thought you knew who I was and why I was here."

"Apology accepted! I apologize for striking back the way I did." I looked at Jane and said, "Jane, you blew it." I gave her a smile and a wink as I said it.

"Jake, there's a reason why I said that's impossible. Although a few people have taken a few pictures of ghost, they're nothing like these," Tasha said holding up the pictures. "And I have never heard of anyone having direct, physical contact with a ghost."

"Doesn't that mean that Peter, at least, is not a ghost?" I asked.

"No, I'm afraid not. What does it mean? I'm not really sure yet," Tasha said. "For some reason, you're the only one who has had contact with the spirits in Slippery Gulch, and of course, this unique contact with Peter."

Smith cut in, "Look, I'm getting sick and tired of hearing about this little brat. We have a case to solve and all this talk about something that doesn't exist anyway is not only ridiculous, it's a waste of time. Where is the crusher?"

"Agent Watson," I said struggling to keep my temper in check, "I feel sorry for you. When this is all over, the rest of us will go our own separate ways. But you have to go back to Reno with her." For the first time, I thought I noticed a slight sign of a smile creep across his face for a quick second.

Before Smith had a chance to respond, Frank said, "Agent Smith, I apologize on behalf of my client. At the present time, my client is suffering from mental duress." In plain English, I assumed he was saying that I was temporarily insane.

Before anyone could go on in that direction, George repeated Smith's question. We all sat quietly pondering the question, where is the crusher. No one had an answer. I just wasn't ready to start thinking about the crusher yet. I finally came up with not an answer, but a comment. "I'm sorry, but I just can't buy into any of this. Peter is not a ghost You're all trying to convince me that he is, based on Lord knows what. I know he isn't. He's not dead. None of you were there. None of you talked to him, touched him, saw those pathetically sad eyes or that beautiful, toothless smile. I'm sorry, but the Peter I saw is not dead."

Everyone looked at George and I did too. Not knowing what to expect, we all waited. George sat there quietly for a couple of minutes collecting his thoughts. "Jake, I'm not sure how I'm going to do this, so excuse me in case I ramble. As you know, several people have seen phantom tracks over the years in that town, Mike being one of them. You are the only one who has seen more than mere tracks. I believe there are two reasons for this: One is the timing. It was exactly 100 years ago to the day that Peabody originally tried to ship the crusher. But something inexplicable happened. Peabody discovered the crusher was missing. Frank theorizes the crusher never left town 100 years ago. Perhaps the driver was distracted long enough for the crusher to be removed and something of similar weight put in its place, like a large rock. If the crusher were covered with a tarp of sorts, the driver would not have known the difference. At any rate, based on what Peter told the driver and was then passed on to Peabody, he approached Stevenson. A fight may have broken out and Peabody was murdered. He died a violent death before completing his task and returned 100 years later to try again. Of course, most of this is speculation but we do know from the record that Peabody was murdered on that day in 1901. Since there were no witnesses, we don't know for certain who the killer was. Logic says that Stevenson was."

"And Peter?" I asked.

George sighed. "Much of what we know is speculation. But we do know from records that Peter was born in Slippery Gulch on December 2, 1895. We also know that his mother died in childbirth. This is all in the town records probably because of the nature of Peter's death but in great detail, owing to the fact that an article appeared in the *Slippery Gulch Gazette* the day after Peter was murdered. I'll let you read it in a minute.

"We believe the driver befriended Peter when he was in town. Or perhaps the driver was from the town himself and already knew Peter. That part is not clear. Peter had been severely beaten by his father on a number of occasions in the past. Again this is eyewitness reporting. Peter was deathly afraid of his father and was seeking help, probably knowing that violence was imminent. But none came.

"You have to remember that back in those days, especially in backwoods communities like this one, what a man did to his wife and family was largely his business. During the fight, Peabody probably told Stevenson how he learned that Stevenson was involved in the disappearance of the crusher. After killing Peabody, Stevenson, in a drunken rage, caught his young son in the middle of the main street, beat him mercilessly to the ground, and brutally finished him off with a knife. Peter died before completing what he had set out to accomplish, namely, saving himself. Thus, 100 years later, he was trying again, just as Peabody was trying again, to successfully complete his task.

"I know this isn't going to be easy, Jake: Here's a copy of the article written about Peter's short life and early death." George handed me the paper. As I read through the article mesmerized, I could have heard a pin drop. It was all here in black and white, all a part of small town history, USA. Peter was dead, murdered by his own father in the middle of Main Street in Slippery Gulch, Montana, in 1901. It was just too incredible! Maybe the child I saw and talked with was a different Peter. Yeah, that had to be it. But I accepted deep down that a boy named Peter was dead.

As if George were reading my mind, he continued to convince me. "One of the many interesting things about all of this is the exact location of Peter's murder. It happened in the street, right in front of Jacob's Mercantile. Now look again at the pictures you have of Peter."

I did. Behind Peter was an old sign on a building barely readable: Jacob's Mercantile. Part of the building could be seen through Peter's body. "Oh my God," I said. "As I was leaving town, Peter stopped me at the exact location of his murder." Chills suddenly ran up and down my spine. "But if Peter is a ghost, why was I able to have physical contact with him? I touched the boy, I held him. I even tickled him. How was that possible?"

George looked at Tasha, who said, "Now it's time for me to do some speculating. As I said earlier, I've never heard of physical contact with a ghost before. Children are different from adults. They tend to be far more open and free than adults are. And the spirits of children tend to be the same way. Peter was desperate and terrified. In life we now know he was abused and neglected, and your pictures confirm that. Apparently, Peter liked and respected the first driver and saw in him a chance for help and possibly an escape. It didn't happen.

"But 100 years later, you came along. He confused you with the first driver. In you he sensed an even stronger interest in his plight than he was shown by the first driver. You obviously liked the boy and showed him a certain amount of affection—possibly the first he'd known in his life. You, of course, thought he was alive. At any rate, the bond was strong enough between the two of you to bridge death itself. I don't understand this myself, but it's the best professional answer I can come up with."

"I'm really getting tired of hearing about this snot-nosed little brat," Smith said. "Where's the crusher?"

"First of all, Ms. Smith," Tasha said, showing emotion for the first time, "ghosts don't produce snot." We all laughed, except for Smith. Even Lurch was laughing this time. The room grew quiet again. Tasha continued. "Second, I think Jake may be able to come up with an answer to the crusher question."

"Now why didn't I think of that?" Smith asked reproachfully. "I suppose he could just look into your crystal ball and magically see the crusher sitting around somewhere."

This time we all just ignored her. "Me?" I said. "Tasha, I have no idea where it is."

"I realize you don't right now, but when we get to town, the bond between you and Peter may prove fruitful. You may be able to reestablish contact with Peter…Peter's ghost, I should say."

"Well, that sounds intriguing. How do you contact a ghost?"

"He'll contact you. Just be natural. Remember, the last time you saw Peter, you saw a very sad and obviously neglected little boy. You showed concern and compassion and gave him affection and friendship. You gave him a reason to smile and laugh. The only thing that has changed is this: Then you thought of him as alive; now you know he isn't!"

I thought about everything I had just heard and read. How could this be? My head was swimming. "Well, okay. All I can be is myself." I asked everybody another question. "If both Peter and Peabody were last alive in the year 1901, why didn't both of them react to the size and noise of my rig?"

"I've been thinking about that myself, Jake," Tasha said. "I can't say for certain. But I believe what you saw and heard were not exactly what they saw and heard. In other words, you saw and heard a truck; they likely saw and heard a freight wagon and a team of horses."

I thought about this for a minute. "That could explain a lot, in itself. The old man I ran into before going up to the mine said something about my old nags. And Peabody said something about the biggest Pittsburgh freighter he'd ever seen. And yes, one other thing: Peter didn't say a word about the truck when I started it."

"I recall that you mentioned Peabody's comment when he saw your trailer," George said. "And something he said about 4,000 pounds being a heavy load. Well, in 1901 that was a heavy load, especially in these mountains."

"Well, let's get going then," I suggested.

"Hold on, Jake, there's more. You've got to hear it," George said.

"Lord, how can there be more?"

"There is, Jake," Frank confirmed. "Have a seat. It gets spookier."

At this time Lurch took over. He took out two pieces of paper and handed both to me. They were copies of the bill of lading. "Mr. Winters, do you recognize these?"

"Sure—the bill of lading. One is the original and one is a rather poor copy."

"And is that your signature on both?"

"Yes, it is."

"Are you sure?"

"Of course, I'm sure."

"Well, the FBI is also," Lurch said. "We had them both analyzed by an FBI handwriting specialist. They compare favorably with your signature on the form you signed in Reno. It is confirmed that all three signatures are yours. But we seem to have a little problem." He pointed to the poor copy. "This is not a poor copy. George found this in the museum and made a copy of it. George took both your attorney and me to see the original. You may notice that both are dated 6-29-01. The problem that we have is that this one"—he pointed to the good copy—"Shows the year as 2001. This one"—he pointed to the poor copy—"is probably dated 1901."

"Wait a minute," I said. "Why do you say 'probably'?"

"Everything in the museum is on record as to date of purchase or date of donation. And by whom. This document was donated to the museum in 1906. The donor was anonymous," Lurch concluded.

"This just doesn't make sense. How could I have signed a form in 1901? I'm older than any of you, but I'm not that old." They chuckled at that one! That is, all except for Smith. She may still have been thinking about ghost snot.

"Am I inferring accurately that the driver of the wagon 100 years ago was also named Jake Winters?"

"That's correct, Mr. Winters," Lurch said.

"Tell me, did you find a tintype picture of the guy also?"

"No, we didn't, but I'd be willing to bet that the similarity between the two of you would be striking," George added. "I believe that is why the bond between you and the boy was so strong."

"Wait a minute," Smith interrupted. "It sounds as if you're buying into all of this bull."

"Smith," Lurch said, "there are some things even the FBI can't explain."

Maybe this guy wasn't so bad after all, I thought.

"This is ridiculous. We're going to allow this criminal suspect to pretend he's made contact with a kid pretending to be a ghost? These people are going to make us look like fools and you're playing right into their little game," Smith said angrily.

"Do you have any better ideas?" Lurch asked Smith.

"Yes, as a matter of fact, I do. Take Winters back to Reno and arrest him for the theft of interstate commerce. Get all of these people out of the investigation; and if they persist, arrest them for obstruction of justice."

"Look, Smith," Lurch said, "at present we have no proof Winters had anything to do with the disappearance of the crusher. In fact, we don't even have any proof the crusher is missing, since we have no firm proof the crusher was ever loaded onto Mr. Winters' truck. The only thing we have is a bill of lading. No, we have two—one from 1901 and one from a week ago. Both are signed by the same individual. Now I'm not saying I believe in ghosts, Ms. Smith, but something strange is going on here and the Bureau will get to the bottom of it. Mark my word."

"May I suggest," Frank said, "that we all adjourn and reconvene at Slippery Gulch? George, Jane, and Mike—you are coming, aren't you?"

"You're darn right we are," Jane said. "I wouldn't miss this for the world."

"Wait a minute," I said. "Frank, did you ever open that letter I gave you from Peabody to his brother?"

"As a matter of fact, I did. All it contains is an apology from Jeremiah to Jacob. That helped the FBI to verify his signature on the bill of lading as legitimate."

"So at one time or another he was at least partially human. That's comforting to know."

## TWENTY-THREE

We all went out and got into two 4-by-4s and in one week's time from my first visit, I was again on my way to Slippery Gulch. The last time I hadn't been sure what I was getting myself into and I felt I was in the same boat today.

When we got to the cliff, I couldn't believe it! It was just as it appeared in the picture and just as George described it. Five feet of the road's width was gone. For 20 feet it was only 4 feet wide, the result of a landslide.

"If this road has been out for months, how was I able to drive my truck across it?" I asked to anyone who happened to have an answer.

"Jake, who knows? I'm not sure if we ever will. And who knows what will turn up in town?" George said. "That's not much of an answer, but what can I say?"

George was right. It wasn't much of an answer.

We walked to the edge of town following the tracks of my truck and many of their tracks from a few days before. We stopped and Tasha said, "Jake, I'd like you to go to the exact spot in front of Jacob's Mercantile where you took the pictures. Be sensitive to a possible contact. The rest of us will stay well hidden. Just remember to be confident you are talking to a living child. Let him know that you've come back to see him. That you worried about him. But play it by ear. You did bring the pictures with you, didn't you?"

"I have them."

"Good. Even if you don't feel you've made contact, show the pictures anyway. Who knows what will happen?"

"Jake," Frank said, "if you do make contact, ask about the crusher."

The rest of the group went into a building across the street from the mercantile while I stood there wondering what to say and how to say it. I'd never knowingly talked to a 6-year-old ghost, or any other ghost for that matter. I still wasn't totally convinced Peter was a ghost. Or maybe I was afraid he was.

I started walking to the mercantile. I acted as natural as possible. About 50 feet from the store, I yelled out, "Hey, Peter, it's me, Jake Winters. I told you I'd be back." There was nothing. I walked to where Peter and I had stood. Both my tracks and some of his were still visible. I turned to where the others were and was about to shrug my shoulders in defeat when once again, there was a small tug on my back pocket. I turned around and there, not standing 2 feet away, was Peter, filthy, skin and bones, just as before.

A big smile came over both our faces at once. I was going to say, "I told you I'd be back," but before I had a chance, he jumped into my arms and said, " I knew you'd be back." Suddenly I realized Hank was right. I was a liar. I was worried about this kid. I put him down, knelt down to his level, ruffled his blond, matted hair, and said, "I knew you weren't a—" I looked over his shoulder and my heart froze. Behind Peter were five small sets of bare footprints in the dirt starting five footprints away and ending where he now stood. How could he do this sort of thing? Unless...

"You knew I weren't what, Jake?"

That took some quick thinking. "I knew you weren't a little brat, like Peabody called you."

He giggled and repeated, "I just knew you'd come back, Jake."

"Well, I said I'd try and here I am. Peter, I've got something to show you. Remember when I took your picture?"

"Yeah, and you had to tickle me?"

"Well I've got them with me." I pulled out the pictures and showed them to him.

He stood there staring at them and finally looked up at me and said, "Is that really me?"

"That's really you, Peter. Pretty good-looking kid, don't you think?" He giggled but saw sadness in my eyes. Now Peter was staring at me questioningly. "Peter, I'm really sorry I wasn't able to help you. I tried but just wasn't able."

"It's okay, Jake. Don't worry about it. At least you came back."

I meant to bring up the crusher, but out came, "Your father really did kill you, didn't he?" I couldn't believe what I was asking.

"I told you he would if he caught me. He's not the one that caught me though. That other guy I told you about caught me. I was walking down that alley and he reached out from a doorway and grabbed me by my shirt. I almost got away. I wiggled out of my shirt, but before I could start running, he grabbed my arm and dragged me out to the street. My daddy was there. I've never seen him that mad. I was real scared. I tried to get away, but the other guy held me. My daddy called me a little bastard and punched me real hard. I fell on the street and was seeing stars. Before I could do anything, he started stabbing me with his knife. Then it was over. It didn't hurt anymore."

I closed my eyes. I felt sick. How could anyone do that to a little kid? I opened my eyes to find Peter staring at me. He gently wiped away a tear. I was embarrassed with my emotions and went on. "Peter, I'm so sorry. I wish there had been something I could have done but now I know, there wasn't. But I have a question: Am I the only person who can see and hear you?"

He nodded.

"Can other people see and hear you if you allowed them to?"

"Yeah, I guess."

"Then why am I the only person?"

"You're fun. I just scare other people. That's fun, but you're the only one that's ever been nice to me."

"Was the first Jake Winters nice to you?"

"He was okay, but he never promised to come back. And he never did. I knew you would."

"How did you know?"

"I don't know, I just did."

"Well, you were right. Peter, why can I touch you?"

He thought for a minute and said, "I don't know. Maybe because I let you."

"One last question, Peter. Do you know where the crusher is?"

"Yeah, don't you?"

"No, where is it?"

"It's in the mine."

"Are you sure?"

"They took it out of your wagon when you were in the office. After that other man walked into the office. You were in there for a long time. While you were in there they took the crusher out and dragged it into the mine and replaced it with a huge rock. And covered it with that big piece of cloth. Then they erased all the tracks. When you came out, it looked like the crusher was still in your wagon."

There never was a piece of cloth in my trailer but I guess that's beside the point. "Who was the other man in the office?"

"He was the mean man who caught me. I don't know his name. Don't you?"

"No, I don't." I now realized he was confusing 1901 with 2001. It was obvious he never did see my truck, only a wagon. "Peter, I have to find that crusher."

"Why?"

"Well, it's kind of hard to explain. Some lawmen think I stole it. If we can find it, then they'll know I didn't steal it."

"I know right where it is. You go back in the mine a ways and there's a fork. When you get to the fork, you go that way," he pointed to his right. "After you go that way, you go a little ways and there's like a small room on that side of the tunnel," again pointing to his right. "It's in there."

"Peter, how do you know all of this?"

"I was hiding behind some bushes. I saw everything. After you left town, I went back up to the mine. I just looked around until I found it. They had it on some kind of wheels. They only erased the tracks in the opening of the main shaft. Once I got to the fork, I could follow the tracks."

"You must have been scared stiff."

"I was scared Daddy or one of the other men was going to catch me. They didn't, not then anyway."

I stood there quietly for a moment. "Peter, you've been a great help. I'd better get going. I've got to get my friends and try and find that crusher. Will I see you again before leaving town?"

"Maybe, but only if you promise me one thing."

"What's that?"

"Would you tickle me real good before you leave?"

I laughed. Most kids must be the same whether they're alive or dead. "I promise. I'll see you in a little while." I moved my fingers as if I were tickling him. Out came that beautiful, toothless smile.

"Promise?"

"I promise. See that alley? That's where I'll meet you." With that, I walked across the street toward an old building. Before going in, I turned around. Peter was gone.

## TWENTY-FOUR

As soon as I walked in, Tasha said, "You did it, didn't you?"

"I did, but you didn't see him, did you?"

"No, but we saw you kneel down. We all knew why."

"It was just like last time. I touched him again, and I got some questions answered." For George's benefit, I explained how a third party caught Peter.

"The paper didn't indicate there was another person involved in Peter's murder," he commented.

"On a lighter note, he also told me where the crusher is."

"You're kidding," Frank said. "Where is it?"

I relayed everything Peter had told me about the crusher. For Tasha's benefit, I relayed everything he told me about himself. I could see quite clearly Smith didn't believe a word of what I said, but for a change, she kept her mouth shut.

Before heading up to the mine, Tasha headed straight for where Peter and I had been, and sure enough, there in the dirt were small, bare footprints starting nowhere and vanishing into thin air. Smith looked at these with great interest but said nothing. Maybe she was starting to come around.

From there we walked up to the mine. The first thing I noticed was the tripod Peabody used to load the crusher. I walked over to it. It was just as George had described. The wood was rotting and the steel parts were rusted severely, to the point that all formerly moving parts were frozen in rust. I stood there in total disbelief. I turned to Tasha. "When a person dies, he can come back as a spirit. But what brings a ruined piece of machinery back new? And then puts it to old?"

"Spirits display an enormous amount of power when trying to accomplish what they have come back for," she said.

"Could that explain why the washed-out road was in good shape when Jake drove over it?" Frank asked.

Tasha thought for a minute and finally said, "I hadn't thought that through. I suppose that could be the answer."

Smith moaned and Lurch said, "Let's see if the kid was right." We all headed for the mine entrance. The entrance was just as you would expect, right out of a 1940s or 1950s Hollywood western movie. The entrance was maybe 6 feet wide and 5 or so feet high, supported by large wooden beams. The inside was dark and forbidding. I could imagine it being full of all kinds of critters.

"Jane, do you have a flashlight in your backpack?" Mike asked.

"Of course, dear," she said with obvious sarcasm in her voice, "I always come prepared." Sure enough, she produced a light.

Tasha said, "I believe I have a small one in my purse." She reached in and produced a light not much larger than a penlight.

"Jane," George said, "I think you and Tasha should stay here."

"Not on your life. I've come this far and I want to see the infamous crusher. Not only that, the flashlights belong to Tasha and me. If we don't go, our lights don't go. Isn't that right, Tasha?" Tasha adamantly agreed, so us men looked at each other, shrugged our shoulders, and followed Jane and Tasha inside. I noticed Smith didn't appear to be too excited about entering. Yet it appeared she didn't want to stay outside by herself either, so she joined us. Maybe she was resigned to the fact a snot-nosed ghost lurked nearby.

The place was musty and dark. The flashlights showed the tracks on the floor of the shaft. They belonged to small, four-legged animals and one small, two-legged animal. It was clear Peter had been here. No adult tracks appeared anywhere. It was plain that most of his tracks had been totally erased by small animal traffic.

"Jake, has Peter been in here since the day they stole the crusher?" George asked.

"He must have been. These tracks wouldn't last for 100 years, would they?"

"In here? I think so. There's no weather in here to destroy the tracks," George said. "Just the tracks of small animals, like what we're seeing."

"So Peter's tracks could have been left by him when he was alive?" Jane asked before I had a chance.

"Very likely," George said.

"That's incredible," I sighed.

"This whole thing is crazy," Smith grumbled.

"Agent," George said, "if you'd like to go back, be my guest." If looks could kill, George would have been dead on the spot.

We continued walking in the shaft until we came to the fork. Everyone looked for Peter's tracks but none could be seen. Both shafts narrowed quite a bit and the animal tracks were concentrated. "Now what, Mr. Winters?" Smith asked sarcastically. "I suppose your imaginary urchin told you which way to proceed?"

I'd just about had enough of this witch. I was about to blow when Frank grabbed my arm. It was just what I needed. I said as civilly as I could, "As a matter of fact, Agent Smith, he did. We go to the right. A ways down, there's a small room or depression in the wall on the right. The crusher will be there."

We walked to the right, keeping an eye out for Peter's tracks, but saw none. Then after what seemed like several hundred feet, we came to a small room, perhaps used for tool storage at one time. Jane peeked around the corner with the help of her light and exclaimed, "Oh my God, it's here!" We all walked into the small opening and just stared. There were the wheel tracks, the adult tracks, and the tracks of Peter again appearing. And there, sitting against the wall was the source of my current problems. It was sitting on some kind of a small, rolling stand.

Frank broke the spell, "Jake, is this it?"

I continued staring. I walked from one end to the other. Since it was against the wall, I couldn't walk around it. It didn't matter. I hadn't paid that much attention to it the week before. There were no distinguishing marks on it that I could recall. Yet I had no doubt this was it! "Yes, Frank. This is it."

Jane was down on her hands and knees looking at it more closely. "How can you be so sure that's the one?" Frank asked.

I shrugged. "I just am. I just know this is the one."

Jane said, "I've been looking at this. I know a little bit about antique mining machinery. This is small for a crusher, designed for a small operation and this was a small operation. Most crushers were 15 to 20 tons. This is 2 tons. There weren't that many made. I'd be willing to bet this is one of the very few of these left. In fact, it may be the only one. That would be easy enough to check on."

"What were you planning to do with it, Mr. Winters?" Smith said.

"Excuse me?" I said.

"I think you heard me, Mr. Winters," she repeated. But before I had a chance to answer, everybody else jumped in.

"Now wait a minute, Ms. Smith," Jane said. "Are you insinuating Jake hid this crusher for some kind of financial gain?"

"It seems rather obvious, doesn't it," Smith said. "He was the driver who supposedly picked up the load. He is the driver who supposedly took it to Reno. And he knew its location."

"You heard him. It was Peter who told him where it was," Mike countered.

"Oh, come on," Smith said. "If you believe that, I've got a bridge I want to sell you. He keeps talking about some little kid no one else can see. Until I see this…this Peter character for myself, he's no more than a figment of Winters' imagination."

That gave me an idea.

"This thing weighs 4,000 pounds, Smith," George said. "Could you explain to all of us how he got that thing in here?"

Very sarcastically, as if George was the most stupid person on earth, she said, "Obviously he had help." I almost missed Lurch roll his eyes.

"How do you explain the fact that Jake drove across a road that had been washed out months earlier?" Frank asked.

"Apparently your geologist friend was wrong," Smith said.

"And obviously, Smith, you're all wet," Lurch said. Smith looked at Lurch in utter shock; the rest of us looked at him in surprise. Lurch was finally standing up to this woman. He continued, "Both you and I walked across that slide, Smith, with the rest of these people. We both walked across the little dried-up stream caused by the spring runoff. And it didn't take a geologist to see that it had been there for quite some time. I don't understand how Mr. Winters got his truck into town, but he did." He paused for a moment. "I really don't understand any of this, but when comparing what we've seen and heard here today with the history of the town, I find it fascinating. Furthermore, I've come to the conclusion that Mr. Winters didn't have anything to do with the disappearance of the crusher. In fact, it never did disappear because here it is."

Smith was seething. "Don't tell me you're buying into Winters' explanation as to how he knew the crusher was here?"

"I've never believed in ghosts before," Lurch said, "but there are things going on here that neither I nor the FBI, I'm sure, can explain. Let's get out of this place. To be perfectly honest, it gives me the creeps."

We all chuckled and agreed. It appeared that Lurch was human after all. We all turned to leave, but before any of us took a step, Tasha yelled, "Stop!" We all jumped but didn't move. Tasha shined her flashlight on the ground behind us up a ways in the entrance shaft. There in the dirt were two small footprints, impressed over ours, as if a small child had been standing there watching us. That was it, just those two. Smith didn't say a word. We walked out of the mine in silence. The brilliant sunlight mocked our darkened minds.

Frank looked at Lurch and said, "Well, Agent Watson, after your little speech inside, I guess you agree the infamous crusher has been found?"

"I'm satisfied," said Lurch.

Before Lurch could go on, Smith fairly yelled out, "What? How can you be? I don't know exactly how Mr. Winters got the crusher from his truck to the mine, but I'm sure he did. And I plan to prove it."

"I don't believe this," Jane muttered.

Lurch was going to say something, but before he could, I said, "Let's go back into town. I may have a way to satisfy even Agent Smith. I don't know if it will work, but I'll try." All but Tasha looked at me slightly puzzled; she threw me a slight smile.

Before going very far, I said, "Wait a minute. I'd like to walk over to the office for a minute." The rest followed. Just as George had said: no horse tracks, just mine and now George's, Jane's, and Frank's. The inside was just as I remembered it. There was no sign anyone had been in there for 100 years except for my one-week-old tracks on the dusty floor. A thought came to me. I walked back outside and said to Tasha, "Look, Peter said that after I walked into the office, another man walked in, apparently to distract me. There was no other man in the office when I was there."

"As you said, you thought Peter may be confusing 1901 with 2001. The man he saw walk into the office was probably acting in 1901."

"But I wasn't in the office more than 2 or 3 minutes, certainly not enough time to get the crusher out of my truck and into the mine." I thought for a moment. "So what you're saying is that perhaps Frank was right all along? What I saw when Peabody was loading my trailer was an apparition? The crusher never made it into my trailer? That just doesn't seem possible. It was so real."

"Nevertheless," Frank said, "I think that's the answer."

"So you're saying Mr. Winters secured nothing more than an apparition?" Smith added.

"That's about the size of it," Tasha said.

"That's about the most asinine thing I've ever heard," Smith said

I had to admit, it did sound like a pretty crazy idea. But I sure didn't have any better ones. When we got back to town, I asked all of them to stay put about 100 feet from a certain alley.

Jane looked at me. "I just made a promise to Peter and now I'm going to keep it."

"Oh, brother." Smith shifted her weight to one leg and rolled her eyes back.

I looked at her, then at Tasha. Although Tasha said nothing, she gave me a knowing tilt of the head. I walked back into the alley and called for Peter. He materialized right in front of me. I really wished he hadn't done that. A chill ran up and down my back. If ever I had a doubt as to what he really was, it was now gone. "I told you it was there," Peter said.

"Yep, you sure did. You were right. You were up there with us, weren't you?"

"Ha-ha!"

"We saw your tracks."

Changing gears, he asked with a certain amount of excitement and anticipation, "Are you going to tickle me?"

"You bet I will. But first, a favor!"

The rest of the group was talking among themselves on the street when they heard screeches, screams, and hysterical, high-pitched laughter emitting from the alley. As relayed to me by Jane on our way back to Basin later, the following conversation took place in my absence.

"What was that?" Smith asked.

"I think that was the sound of a very special type of bonding between the worlds of the mortal and the immortal," Tasha said.

"Or maybe it was the sound of Jake's overactive imagination," Frank volunteered. Everybody laughed except Smith.

"What do you think Jake has up his sleeve?" Jane asked.

"I'm not really sure," Tasha said, watching the alley for me to walk out alone, "But I think we're about to find out."

Still smiling broadly, I took Peter's hand as we walked up to the group of people waiting for me. I looked on the ground behind me but my tracks were the only ones visible. I walked right in front of Agent Smith. "What was going on back there?" Frank asked. "We heard all kinds of yelling and screaming and it obviously wasn't you."

"You heard that?" I asked, wondering how. While they nodded their heads, I said, "I promised Peter I'd tickle him before I left. But I don't understand how you heard him."

Smith said, "Oh for Pete's sake, Winters, give us a break. I don't know what you're up to but—"

I interrupted her and said, "Agent Smith, it gives me great pleasure to introduce you to, Peter Stevenson." With that, I let go of his hand and that was the signal. Peter materialized before their eyes, letting out a bloodcurdling scream and jumping right at Smith. She let out with a scream of her own and landed on her derriere. The effect I'd hoped for was perfect. Peter was laughing hysterically. He looked at me and said, "Did I do good, Jake?"

"Oh yeah, Peter," I said ruffling his filthy hair. "You sure did." I bent over and whispered in his ear, "Could you stay visible to these people for just a few more minutes?" He nodded yes.

A laughing Lurch and Frank helped Smith up. Smith, staring at Peter, with eyes the size of silver dollars, appeared to be in shock. The rest appeared to be in a state of disbelief...well, all except Tasha. She seemed to understand.

"Peter, before you go," I said, "I want you to meet three people who were also worried about you. They live only a short distance from here."

I put my hand on his shoulder and led him to George. I said, "Peter, do you remember when I put that thing up to your ear and you heard someone inside talking to you?"

"Yeah."

"Well, that was this guy here. This is George."

"Wow!" Looking up at George, Peter said, "How did you get in there?"

We all laughed. George stuck out his hand to shake Peter's, but his hand passed right through. George stopped laughing real quick and turned ghost-white, and a little peaked. Peter said, "I forgot, George. I'm sorry, but Jake is the only one who can touch me."

George recovered quickly and said, "That's okay, Peter. It's a great honor just to finally meet you."

We moved on to Mike. "Peter, this is Mike, George's brother-in-law. In other words, Mike married George's sister. He was up here a few years ago. While here he saw a few of your footprints, the kind that start no place and end in thin air. You scared the living daylights out of him!"

"I did?" Peter said, great emphasis coming through his words.

Mike leaned down toward Peter and faked being mad. "You sure did, kid. I left town real quick." Peter looked scared. For a moment I feared he might vanish. Mike continued with a smile. "Now that I've had the privilege of meeting you, I can't think of anyone I'd rather be scared by. You did a great job."

Peter suddenly showed pride in himself, displaying his beautiful smile and simply saying, "Thank you."

He and I then went on to Jane. "Peter, this is Jane, George's sister. And she's Mike's wife. She was also very concerned about you."

"You were?" Peter intoned.

Jane went to her knees and was about to give him a hug. I caught her attention and she held back. Between my accounts of Peter, the newspaper accounts of his short life and tragic death, my pictures of him, and now the real thing, it looked like Jane's tear bubble was about to burst. She said, "I sure was. The three of us were up here looking for you the day after Jake was here, but we didn't see you anywhere. Why didn't you scare us?"

He put his head down and hesitated. He touched his index finder to his grimy cheek. Then looking up at Jane, he said, "I knew you were friends of Jake's, so I didn't want to scare you. If I did, I thought Jake might get mad at me and not come back." He paused for a minute, lowered his head again, then added just above a whisper, "Jake is the only friend I've ever had."

That did it! Jane couldn't hold back the floodgates. Her tears flowed freely, and I had a lump in my throat. Peter looked at me and said in a sad voice, "I didn't mean to hurt her."

"You didn't, Peter," Jane said through her sobs. "I just feel so sad we weren't able to help you." He didn't know what to say and the rest of us didn't either. Jane broke the silence: "How did you know we were Jake's friends?"

"I heard you talking about him."

"Peter, I'd love to be able to give you a big hug but I know I can't, so could Jake give you a hug for me?"

Peter smiled at Jane, then at me and said, "Okay." He turned to me and I picked him up and gave him a quick hug. Then Peter let out with a loud squeal and irresistible giggle.

"What was that all about?" Jane asked.

"Oh, sorry. I kind of got a finger stuck between two of his ribs," I said and we all laughed.

He again looked at Jane, then back at me and said, "She's pretty."

"She sure is," I said, "and she doesn't look anything like George, does she?" George had a smile on his face. I again tickled Peter to produce another giggle, put him down, and said, "Let me introduce you to the rest of my friends."

Tasha was totally amazed by this entire exchange. Smith was in a state of shock but was coming around. When we got to Smith, Peter said, "Is she your friend, too?"

I looked at Smith and said, "Yes."

"Why is she wearing those funny glasses, Jake?" he asked innocently. Leave it to a child.

Before I had a chance to answer, Smith said, "Well if a ghost thinks so...when I get home, I'm going to get a different pair." Smith actually smiled at Peter.

"Guess what, Peter?" I put in. "We have to get going. Why don't you put on a show for these people and disappear before you and I go back to the alley for a couple of minutes."

"Will you tickle me one more time?"

Everybody chuckled and I said, "Sure, why not. Here or there?"

"There," he said pointing to the alley and instantly disappeared to everybody except me. I took his hand and said to everyone, "I'll be back in a few minutes, folks." Peter and I walked off, both of us leaving our own set of prints, for about five feet; then there was only one set.

While I was saying my final and emotional goodbye to Peter, the rest of the group was talking among themselves. The following conversation was relayed to me by Jane, George and Mike.

Mike said, "You know, Peter is really a neat little kid. He sure was proud of himself when I told him how scared I was a few years ago."

They all laughed. George said, "Yeah, he is, Mike. One thing I don't understand. He's such a polite, well-mannered, and caring little kid. With such a jerk for a father and apparently nobody showing him any love or affection, how did he turn out so well?"

"First of all," Jane corrected, "he's not a little kid, he's a little ghost. Second, the interest and affection he is now being shown by all of us may bring out the best in him. We are the only ones who know of Peter's existence. I think we should keep it among ourselves. I think we owe that to both Slippery Gulch and Peter."

After some thought, Tasha said, "What we've seen and heard here today could certainly be exploited by any one of us for personal and economic gain. To be quiet, we're giving up on that idea. I agree with you, Jane. If word ever gets out about Slippery Gulch and Peter, and what Peter really is, every nutcase in the country will head here. This secret must remain ours."

Just at that moment, they all heard screeches, screams, and high-pitched laughter coming from the alley. They all looked at each other, with knowing eyes.

A few moments later I emerged from the alley and joined the group. They became quite serious. I said, "Did I miss something?"

Finally Agent Smith spoke up: "Mr. Winters, and the rest of you. I know I've been a burr under every saddle here. I've been a pain and I apologize. I honestly believed Peter was a figment of Jake's imagination. I certainly didn't believe in ghosts. As an employee of the U.S. government, I couldn't and keep my credibility. I don't have a choice now, do I?" Everybody in one way or another comforted Agent Smith. Then she added, "Did he have to scream so loud when he jumped at me?"

"It could have been worse," I said. "He wanted to appear to you as he did after his father murdered him, but I talked him out of that."

"Hey, wait a minute," Mike said. "Has he ever appeared that way to anyone?"

"He said the last time he did it, it was really effective. He told me that some big kids came into town yelling and swearing and throwing rocks through windows so he…"

Mike interrupted. "I think I can finish it. The two kids were basically raising hell. But then fro
m behind them, they heard someone asking for help. They turned around to see a little boy walking toward them. He was naked except for a tattered pair of pants. He was covered with blood. His left hand was holding his intestines in place and a bloodied right hand was stretched out to them. The boy was staggering toward them saying in an unusually deep voice for such a little boy, 'Help me!' As they approached to help, the lad disappeared. But his tracks continued coming toward them, as was an unearthly voice saying, 'Help me! Help me!' They turned around and never ran as fast as they did that day. They jumped in their car and took off, never again to return to Slippery Gulch."

Standing in the middle of the street, we were laughing hysterically picturing the scene. "I just can't picture a cute little boy like Peter doing such a thing," Jane said.

Mike, George, and I looked at each other. "I can," Mike said in all earnestness. George and I both laughed and agreed with Mike.

"When those kids fled in their car, Peter saw only a turn-of-the-century buckboard. How do you know this?" I asked.

"One of those teenagers was a great uncle of mine. He was always making up stories when we were kids. I figured that was just another one of them, until now."

Frank interrupted, "Does this mean my client is in the clear?"

"This investigation is off," Lurch said, "even though I don't know how I'll justify it with the bureau."

"Don't worry about it, agent," Tasha said. "I'm the expert here. I think you're making the right decision."

"We'll figure something out on the way back to Basin," Jane added. "By the way, Jake, do you think you'll ever come back to Slippery Gulch?"

"I don't have a choice. Peter made me promise, and the last thing I want is a ticked off, 106-year-old ghost chasing me around the country. Let's head back to Basin."

"Jake, if any one of the three of us comes back to Slippery Gulch, do you think he will allow us to see or talk to him again?" Jane asked.

"I'm really not sure. I am sure he'll let you know, one way or another, that he is aware of your presence. Mike, he did say he wouldn't scare you again. He liked you teasing him. You made his day. You made him feel proud of himself."

"I think we should get up here in the next two or three weeks. See what happens! Let him know we have not forgotten him."

Tasha said, "I think he would be glad to see any of us again, even if he doesn't appear to us. I have to agree with Jake though, somehow, he'll let us know of his existence."

"I just hope he does it gently," Jane said with a chuckle.

"He knows who all of you are now and knows that you're friends. I don't think you'll have to worry," I said.

As we turned to leave, we heard a rustling in the dirt behind us. There was a small set of footprints heading off in the direction of the old alley. But after a half dozen or so, there were no more.